Gang Girl

Gang Girl

Nancy Miller

James Lorimer & Company Ltd., Publishers
Toronto

James Lorimer & Company Ltd., Publishers acknowledges funding support from the Ontario Arts Council (OAC), an agency of the Government of Ontario. We acknowledge the support of the Canada Council for the Arts, which last year invested $153 million to bring the arts to Canadians throughout the country. This project has been made possible in part by the Government of Canada and with the support of the Ontario Media Development Corporation.

Cover design: Shabnam Safari
Cover image: iStock

Library and Archives Canada Cataloguing in Publication

Miller, Nancy, 1943-, author
        Gang girl / Nancy Miller.

(SideStreets)
ISBN 978-1-4594-1288-0 (softcover).--ISBN 978-1-4594-1289-7 (EPUB)

        I. Title. II. Series: SideStreets

PS8626.I4527G36 2018   jC813'.6   C2017-906497-5
                                               C2017-906498-3

Published by: Distributed in Canada by: Distributed in the US by:
James Lorimer &   Formac Lorimer Books   Lerner Publisher Services
Company Ltd., Publishers   5502 Atlantic Street   1251 Washington Ave. N.
117 Peter Street, Suite 304 Halifax, NS, Canada   Minneapolis, MN, USA
Toronto, ON, Canada   B3H 1G4   55401
M5V 0M3   www.lernerbooks.com
www.lorimer.ca

Printed and bound in Canada.
Manufactured by Friesens Corporation in Altona, Manitoba, Canada in December 2017.
Job # 239691

*This book is dedicated to all teens
who struggle to 'fit in.'
Be careful what you wish for.*

Chapter 1

First Day

Sasha watched the girl standing next to the man. Both were holding on to the hanging straps as the bus swayed back and forth. The girl's well-formed backside seemed poured into her black jeans, and the man's gaze kept flicking over it. Even pulled back into a neat bun, the girl's bright red hair stood out among the greys, blacks, and browns of the morning commute.

Without warning, the bus lurched to a stop. The girl put her hand on the man's chest to steady herself. Glad to have her attention, he leaned on her shoulder and waved off her apology. Sasha saw the girl's other hand discreetly dip into the man's pocket, pull out a wallet, and drop it into her own pocket. Then the girl waved goodbye to the man and got off the bus. It took all of about five seconds and, in that time, Sasha never once saw the thief's face.

Stunned, Sasha almost didn't realize that this was her stop too. When she got off the bus she saw the girl heading for Sasha's brand new school. Sasha looked back and caught the man leaning down to leer at both of them through the bus window.

What a way to start school in a brand new city and country! It wasn't like she wasn't aware of pickpockets. But this, according to her mother, was one of the better areas of Toronto. In Moscow, petty theft was confined to the poorer areas. Sasha had never lived in a poor area, ever.

Of course, back in Moscow her father

had made sure bodyguards were watching the family all the time. Her parents had always worried she would be robbed, kidnapped, or worse. Once she got into her teens, Sasha had tried to duck her guards. She and her friends had gotten away with quite a lot. If only she'd been more careful about that one little hacking job. Just one stupid thing and now here she was in Canada.

Actually, it wasn't just that one stupid thing, she was realizing. She had been getting careless. Every online prank had become less and less of a thrill. She really didn't want to be tied up in a life of crime. Her banishment to Canada may have come at a perfect time for her. She'd saved face with her friends and she got to think about a real future.

The girl on the bus was an eye-opener, though. That wasn't something she expected to see on her first day. But as she arrived at the school, Sasha saw no sign of the girl and she quickly forgot about it.

Sasha was directed to a classroom where all the kids were shouting and throwing things at each other. This would not have happened at home. The teacher stood there, hands on hips. Finally everyone settled down and the teacher turned to Sasha, standing in the doorway. She waved Sasha in and pointed to an empty desk. To get there, Sasha had to walk across the room in front of the whole class and halfway down the other side.

When Sasha was seated, the teacher said, "Class, this is Sasha. She's new to Canada from Moscow. Please help her with her English and anything else. And if you're lucky, maybe she'll help you with your math and computer skills. She's a whiz."

"You can help me with my math anytime," called out one guy, pointing to Sasha and then to himself.

A girl across from him threw a piece of rolled-up paper at him. "Shut up, Max," she said.

Another guy shouted, "Yeah, I could use some computer help. How about we Snapchat with each other?" he said with his fingers tickling the air. Everyone laughed.

It always happened. Sasha was too tall and too blond. She had the physical assets to attract attention — often the wrong kind of attention. Now her face got hot and a drop of sweat rolled down her chest. At home those boys would be punished. Here, the teacher just turned to the board. "Okay class, quiet down and open your books to page one hundred and ten."

What book? What subject?

Sasha quickly sorted through the books she'd been given the week before. She found the one that matched what she saw other kids opening and turned to page 110. She kept her head down, pleading silently, *please don't call on me for anything*. This was just what she was afraid of — being singled out, even ridiculed. Her accent was strong and she knew a lot of

Canadians saw Russian girls as too big and likely on steroids. Her training for basketball and track in Russia had gotten her in shape. But was it the right shape for Canada?

In Moscow, her father's position as a minister of justice made her part of privileged society. It made sure she wasn't centred out or put in the spotlight unfairly. If she wanted attention, she could get it herself. Here, attention needed to come slowly so she could figure out the system.

When the bell rang, everyone rushed out of their seats and out of the room. Sasha was left alone with the teacher, whom she'd never met and whose name she didn't know. She went up to the desk at the front.

"Can you tell me what the homework is, please?" asked Sasha.

"You need to talk to the ESL coordinator — that's English as a second language," said the teacher, handing her a page with typed instructions. "He'll help you make sense of it.

After your last class today, take these papers to him. His office is down the hall and up the stairs on the left. Don't go right or you'll end up in the gym. At the top of the stairs, head past the washrooms to room two thirty-four."

"Thank you . . ." Sasha said, then mumbled, "I guess." She checked her agenda and made her way to her second class.

Chapter 2
The CREW

At the end of the day, with everything she had collected from all her classes, Sasha did her best to remember the directions to find room 234. When she finally arrived, the man behind the desk stood up.

"I'm Frank, the ESL coordinator," he said. "I assume you're Sasha. Ms. Riker told me you were coming."

He held his hand out. Sasha pulled one of her hands from under her stack of books and papers. As she reached out to shake his hand and tried to remember the name *Ms. Riker* at the same time, her books started to topple. She grabbed them, leaving Frank with his hand uselessly hanging in between them. He blushed and laughed a little awkwardly.

"Clumsy. Sorry," Sasha mumbled.

Totally uncomfortable, she sat down in the chair across from his desk while he circled to the other side of it. She dropped her books on another chair, and clutched the papers in one hand. Frank went on. "As the ESL coordinator, my job is to advise new students on their studies and how they can learn better English. Hand me those papers and we'll sort your work."

Before Frank could even sit down, a ripple of laughter from the hall made them both look up. Four girls had crowded themselves into the doorway. Three were standing, one was in a wheelchair. All four wore sweatshirts that said *The CREW.*

"Hey, Frank," said a smoky voice. Sasha turned her head to look at its owner. The girl's buttoned-up grey blouse under her sweatshirt was a little short in the sleeves, and part of the hem on her black skirt was unravelled. Her outfit reminded Sasha of a private school uniform.

The girl announced with great authority, "We've come for your signature on a petition to fence in that dog park across the street."

Instead of taking charge, Frank blushed and sat down. She watched as the girls came closer. She could tell that it made Frank more uncomfortable. "Not now, girls. I'm busy," he tried.

Ignoring him, another girl spoke. She was standing behind the others, so Sasha couldn't see her. But her English accent stood out. "Some of the students have to walk across the park and are afraid of dogs."

Then a third, childlike voice added, "And some of the neighbours are afraid too. We've gone around and we have almost five hundred signatures. How about signing?"

The girl in the wheelchair pushed her way up to Frank's desk. Her confidence shone through as her long, dark hair floated around her pretty face. She put her hand on his arm.

"Oh, come on, Frances," Frank said, moving her hand off his arm. "Please, girls." His discomfort reminded Sasha of how she'd felt in the classroom. "I'm in a meeting now. Come back when I have more time."

The girls pressed on. "Come on, Frank. It will only take a minute."

And the smoky-voiced girl said, "You know you want to."

Another piped in, "Or I could come back when you're alone." The other girls giggled.

"No, thanks."

Then one of them, the tiny girl with the childlike voice, moved around to crouch beside Sasha. Her crisp pink dress was in high contrast to the other girl's shabby uniform. "Hi, Sasha." How did they know her name?

"I saw you in Ms. Riker's class today. I'm Anzuela." She went on to explain to Sasha what the petition was for.

Sasha looked at Frank for help. He threw his eyes to the ceiling and signed as they held out the clipboard. Sasha signed too. The girls quickly left the room. Frank sighed again and his voice was tight. "Shall we get back to work?"

Sasha pulled her courage together. She asked, "Who are they?"

"Ah . . . they are the CREW." Frank shook off his discomfort. "They rule the school as self-appointed leaders. They get away with this kind of stuff because they organize charity events and help people. If Anzuela said you should be involved, believe me, you will be involved."

Sasha's nerves jumped up a notch. Involved?

"But watch out," Frank warned her. "They are pushy. When they want something, they usually get it." He shook his head again and picked up Sasha's papers.

After Frank had explained her homework, Sasha headed out to the hall and tried to retrace her steps to get to the front door. She went down a set of stairs, only to find herself in a brand new hallway. Too late, she realized she'd taken the wrong stairs. And coming toward her was Anzuela, one of the CREW. The girl was smiling, walking in front of a group of students who seemed to be congratulating her on running a great campaign. Anzuela saw her and called out to Sasha, "Come to the gym! See how you can do more."

One guy in the group turned his eyes toward Sasha. "Hey, haven't seen you before." His eyes scaled her body. "You are *fiiine*." The guy who called out to her this morning in class turned to his friend and said, "Out of your league, Freddie. She was in my class this morning. She's from Moscow and she's a little full of herself."

Full of myself, Sasha thought. The slang here was going to be her downfall. Grammar she could do, but "full of herself"? She'd have to learn quickly so she could fit in.

To avoid the other students' stares, Sasha followed the group into the gym. It was crowded with kids and she quickly realized this was the meeting they had been talking about in Frank's office. She started to leave. But the posters and signs around the room caught her eye.

You can be part of the CREW:

Confident

Remarkable

Excellent

Welcoming

All four CREW members she saw earlier stood at the front of the room. Sasha remembered Frances and Anzuela from the ESL office. The girls' name tags identified the others — Martha was the smoky-voiced leader and Beryl was the one with the English accent. Sasha slipped into an empty chair. What could it hurt?

"What does the CREW stand for?" Martha shouted at the students. The crowd shouted back, "Confident, Remarkable, Excellent, Welcoming!" With her jacket off and her sleeves rolled up, Martha had gone from private school student to protest leader.

"Everyone can make the world a little better," she went on. "We all can be leaders." Then Anzuela went around the room with a tablet that showed pictures of a playground, with Anzuela waving at the camera. "This is in Alliston, north of Toronto. My friend asked us to help them get a playground. So the CREW went to work and raised money and wrote letters to officials. In a year, they had a playground."

A second picture showed Frances raking a garden from her wheelchair. Frances wheeled herself to the front of the group. "This is the community garden in Etobicoke that we worked on. It was dying and the CREW rounded up a bunch of people to work it back to health."

Then Beryl came forward holding a laptop. "Using a computer is easy for us," she started. "It's just one of our everyday tools. But for older people who didn't grow up with computers, it's often really complicated. They need our help." She told the group about a seniors' home nearby that was looking for someone to help residents learn basic computer navigation. Her eyes scanned the crowd. "People like you, Sasha." She pointed to Sasha at the back of the room. "I know you've got the computer smarts."

What? This was making her nervous, like a sci-fi movie where everyone knows your name. Or worse, one where everyone wants something from you. Come on. It was only her first day.

But the CREW seemed very popular.

And she did want friends. She needed time to think about it. Her confusion must have shown because, before she could answer, she heard Anzuela's baby voice saying, "It's okay, Sasha, we'll talk to you later. Just keep Friday night open."

The meeting ended and Sasha scurried out the door. Everything was happening so fast. The CREW, the guys coming on to her, the pickpocket on the bus.

Her mother wasn't home when she got there, so she went straight to her room to make sense of her homework. Fortunately, she'd done her math homework at school. The math was easy, far below where she'd been in Moscow.

She let herself think about the CREW. Maybe these *were* the people who ran things. Her father had always said not to get in with troublemakers and to stick to the upper class. But her mother said to find out who's in charge and make friends with them.

For the moment, Sasha thought that her mother knew best.

Chapter 3

New Best Friends

The next day at lunch, Sasha sat alone studying British authors. A deep voice interrupted her thoughts. "Can I sit here?"

Sasha really didn't want anyone there. She needed to study. She frowned and looked up into an electric smile. White teeth and a little lift on one side of perfect lips pointed up into large eyes so dark they were almost black. Those eyes were looking at her like there was nobody else in the room. The boy's coffee-coloured skin was as smooth as a baby's. "Please?" he added.

Sasha hadn't had time to think about guys since she arrived. With her studies and getting used to a new city and school, she was too caught up to hook up.

So what went on here? Was it okay to talk to a boy without being introduced? In Moscow she did it all the time on her own, but that didn't make it acceptable. But he was so cute. And this was different because Sasha recognized him. He was a star basketball player for the school's senior team. She had noticed his picture was in the trophy case and that everyone said hi to him in the halls.

Sasha gestured to the other side of the table. "Go ahead." So much for British authors.

"My name's Jake," he said, taking his seat. "I know yours is Sasha. I have to admit I've been checking up on you."

Sasha's radar clicked in. Maybe he was a spy for her father or for school security. "That sounds creepy," she said. "Why would you do that?"

"Well, so I could learn about you. And I learned you're tall and beautiful, and you play basketball. And you're reading British authors, my favourite subject. Here you are all by yourself. It was the perfect chance to talk to you. So can I talk to you, Sasha?"

Sasha listened, her heart floating up to her throat. She swallowed hard and looked around. Nobody was watching, so she squeaked out a weak, "I guess." Then, getting more confident, she said, "What do you want to talk about?"

"Well, maybe what you're doing Saturday night." Before Sasha could answer, a backpack landed heavily on the table between them. "I know what you're doing Saturday night, Jake," said Martha. "We're all going to the Playground where there's a really sick party and vinyl launch."

"Uh, I don't think so, Martha. There'll be drinking there and I can't party like that. Training, you know. Anyway, I gotta go," he said getting up. "Sasha, we'll have that talk another time, okay?" He turned his bright smile on Sasha and walked off.

When he was gone, Martha looked at Sasha. "Just be careful around Jake. You don't want to make enemies." She smiled and walked away.

What did that mean? Well, it was only her second day. She was sure Jake's interest wouldn't last. Too bad. He seemed really nice.

✹✹✹

The next morning Sasha's mother woke her with a swish of the curtains to let in the light. Covering her eyes with one hand and throwing off the blankets with the other, Sasha sat up.

"So how was school, my darling?" Sasha's mother asked. She hadn't come home until after midnight.

"Different," said Sasha, getting out of bed. "You were home late." Her mother ignored

Sasha's chiding and went digging through Sasha's closet. "Hmmm," her mother said as she scanned the clothing.

"Mother, please do *not* choose my clothes for me," Sasha said. "I know what I'm going to wear. I'll be down in a minute." Sasha closed her closet door, almost catching her mother's hand. Then she stormed into the bathroom.

"Oh, so grouchy. We will see what you choose. Can you tell me one thing about your two days in school?"

"Okay, I met some girls who run a leadership group and they want me to join them."

Her mother actually clapped her hands. "Wonderful. What do their fathers do?"

Sasha came out of the bathroom and checked her closet. "I have no idea," she said. She frowned at her Russian wardrobe. She'd seen what the girls were wearing. And now she was sure she didn't have anything that worked. Jeans with another sweater — a bulky sweater to hide her "assets." She could get away with that for now.

"Oh no," her mother cried when she went downstairs. "That is just awful."

"Mother, it's what everyone wears. I don't want to be singled out. I can choose my own clothes. I'm sixteen."

"Your father would not agree. But I won't tell him if you promise to come with me to the Petrovs' on Friday night. *And* wear something pretty."

Thinking fast, Sasha said, "There's a meeting of those popular girls I told you about on Friday night. I think they like me. And I want to get in with the leaders of the school. Maybe I should go." As her mother compared the benefits of the Petrovs and the student leaders, Sasha ran upstairs to grab her books.

Sasha kept her head down during that first week. So much was happening so fast. She figured out how to read her schedule. She signed up for an advanced ESL course. She surfed the web for the latest clothes. Jake said "hi'" all the time and started coming around her locker in the morning. The CREW hadn't said any more about Friday. And her mother was on her about the Petrovs' party.

On Friday morning on her way to class, she ran into a wall of CREW. All four girls were waiting outside her classroom. Sasha recognized them, but this was her chance to look at them up close.

Martha again led the pack. She was tall with sleek dark hair caught loosely at the back. This time her uniform style was a navy blue pencil skirt and blue blazer. Her eyes floated over Sasha. When Sasha stared back, Martha shifted from wide-open curiosity to squinty suspicion. "Somebody's got money," she said. "Are those Guess jeans?" Her voice sounded like she'd been smoking for years.

Sasha passed her eyes quickly across Martha's outfit. With her mother's eye for clothing details, she noticed Martha's jacket was a little frayed at the cuffs.

Figuring Martha was trying to make

friends, Sasha said, "No, they're Russian knock-offs. I could get you some cheap."

"Do you think I need knock-offs?" Martha snapped.

"No, of course not. I just meant . . ."

Before it went any further, Anzuela cut in, "Hi, Sasha. Remember me?"

Martha said, "More to the point. Do you remember us?" She was definitely the leader.

Sasha nodded.

"Okay, Zorro, you're her control, so give her the details. Tonight, seven o'clock." Then she turned to Sasha. "Oh, a reminder," she said. "I don't think Jake is available. You wouldn't want to step on someone's toes."

They all walked away except Anzuela. The tiny girl said, "We're having a meeting tonight to discuss ways we can volunteer and raise money for good causes. Can you come? The seniors' computer thing is a real opportunity for us — to help, of course."

Good! It would get Sasha out of going to

the Petrovs'. And Sasha could check out the
CREW more closely.

"Sure," she said. "Where? And who's Zorro?"

"Oh, that's me." Anzuela said. "I'll explain
later when I pick you up. I've got a car.
What's your address and phone number?" She
pointed to Sasha's cell. "I'll text when I'm out
front." Sasha wrote down her information and
Anzuela put it into her phone.

"I should take yours too," Sasha said.

"Uh, not right now. I have a couple of
phones, one for CREW business and one
for everything else. Everyone in the CREW
does. This is my business phone. I'll put
your information into my private one too.
See you later."

Sasha went through the rest of the day in
a daze. Both her parents would be impressed
if she made powerful friends in the first week.
She couldn't wait until tonight.

Chapter 4

Stepping Up

Sasha headed to her Political Thinking class, wondering how different it would be from the politics classes at home. Did she miss Moscow? She wasn't sure. She liked the free way the kids acted and talked to the teachers here. It was a little disrespectful but more equal. In Russia, the teachers were always making fun of kids in front of everyone. They never talked to them as adults.

Everyone here seemed to have more fun.

Sasha actually looked forward to going to school every day.

She kind of missed her father, although she'd never seen him much. They had promised to Skype on the weekend, so she would talk to him the next day. Sasha didn't know exactly what her father did in his office as a minister of justice. But sometimes he could be a little scary with his loud voice and threats to "remove" this person and that one. Sasha knew to stay out of his way when a scandal in the government came up. It usually meant his position was in question.

Social media criticism from outside Russia was the worst. One tweet from an American said: *The story is that he can get you anything for a big enough payoff.*

Another story that had swirled around was a controversy from the Russian Consulate here in Toronto. Somehow it involved her father. But that had been months ago, long before she'd even known she'd be moving here.

Her friends in Russia believed her father was evil. They thought everyone in government was evil. They talked all the time about how they could be the ones to topple the corrupt government. But they hung around her because of her father's money and influence. And because, with her talent, they were able to find out all kinds of things. They (Sasha, really) hacked the computers of rich and famous Russians and used the information to damage reputations and make up scandal — anything to embarrass celebrities.

Sasha's one true friend was Kristina. She was another minister's daughter and understood the pressure Sasha was under. But unlike Sasha, Kristina didn't get herself into trouble.

Sasha had never gotten into really bad trouble until two months ago. What had finally her sent away was hacking into the personal files of the prime minister of Russia. Sasha had found out the old guy was messing around with a young woman — definitely not his sixty-year-old wife. In fact, the up-and-coming ballet star was only eighteen years old.

Her friends had loved it. This was top information. Maybe this was just the bit they needed to embarrass the government.

Sasha's father had got wind of the hack just before the scandal went viral. Sasha's friends had posted it on a Russian gossip news site. But her father told her that all the posts had been removed before they went further. The rumour was that her friends had been taken to a quiet, isolated place. Her father said they would not be seen for a long time. Sasha had never seen him so angry.

So that was the punishment for them all — except Sasha. Her father's position made it possible to wipe her record clean and banish her to Canada with her mother for two years. The others were still in jail as far as she knew. Sasha didn't know much about North American prisons except from American movies. But Russian jails, from what she'd heard, were much, much worse. She was thankful she was here instead of in a small, dirty place, cut off completely from everyone and everything. But when she thought of her former friends, her luck at being her father's daughter made her feel guilty.

In laying out the rules before she'd left for Canada, her father had told her she needed to become more serious.

"You need twenty-four-hour watching and your mother will be in charge. If you act out, I will put bodyguards on you. I don't care if it's the custom in Canada or not." He told her that with better English and experience in international living, maybe — just maybe — she'd be able to make something of herself.

Sasha had wondered at the time: why Canada? Why not Europe, or even another part of Russia, as long as it was away from her friends? The story about the controversy in the Russian Consulate in Canada flickered through her mind. Whatever it was, Sasha knew that everything her father did had a purpose for *his* good.

Kristina had told her there were whispers throughout Moscow's elite about why Sasha and her mother were going away. But nothing was ever published.

Her mother never discussed her father's job. Once, when Sasha asked her about a "corruption" comment she'd overheard, her mother had said, "Don't listen to such garbage. Whatever he does for work is not our concern. He takes care of us. That's what is important."

That didn't really satisfy Sasha, but she didn't really care. She lived off her father's actions and his money. And she'd rather be here than in prison with her friends. It was a constant reminder that if she messed up, she could be there with them.

Luckily, her mother had her own agenda here: parties, shopping, and other social events. So she wasn't as attentive as her father thought. Sasha was allowed some freedom, especially when it involved the CREW.

That morning her mother had told her she wanted to take Sasha shopping. Sasha had plucked the credit card out of her mother's hand and said she had a friend from school she would go with. Alone at the mall after school, Sasha looked at what the other girls were wearing. Jeans, leggings, tops cut low in the front, or up above the belly button. Hair mostly long and straight, sometimes cut short and shaved on one side. And so many clothes in one place. How could you choose?

She got home two hours later to find her mother pacing the living room. She grabbed Sasha by the shoulders. "Where were you? Your father called. Who is that friend?"

Finally she stepped back and looked at her daughter. "What have you done to your beautiful curls?"

"Mother, I just had my hair straightened. This is how the other girls have their hair and I want to fit in. And I bought some clothes too. Do you want to see?" She ran with her packages up to her room.

"I don't know. You are changing every day. How can I trust you?" her mother called after her.

When Sasha came down again, her tight black leggings and grey T-shirt that ended at her midriff dropped her mother into a chair. Her mother was speechless, something Sasha had never seen before. Before she could say anything, Sasha ran upstairs again, shouting, "You'll like this one better!" This time, high leather boots and a leather skirt to mid-thigh showed off Sasha's long legs.

"And now something for you, Mother," she called before descending a third time. She wore a blue floral dress that ended just above her knees. It had short, flowing sleeves and straps crossing her back. Her mother just nodded and went to her own room, probably to complain to her father.

But now she had clothes and friends. Sasha was sure she would fit in.

Chapter 5

Different Names, Different Games

At 7:00 p.m., Anzuela's text came. "I'm leaving now," Sasha called to her mother. Wearing her new leather boots and skirt, she figured she looked perfect for the meeting.

Outside, a cute little Smart car was pulled up. After getting in and putting on her seat belt, Sasha looked over at her new friend with a smile that quickly faded. Cute little Anzuela was now dressed in very short shorts and tight, layered tank tops. The one on the outside said *Bring it on*.

Anzuela stomped on the gas pedal and the tires squealed. "We don't want to be late," she said. "Master doesn't like it when we're late."

They parked in front of a mansion. It was dark except for faint light coming out of the window of the front room. Sasha followed Anzuela and noticed that those shorts revealed shapely and very adult legs. Anzuela knocked on the door with a tap-tap, pause, tap-tap. Beryl opened the door, checked around the neighbourhood, and closed it behind the three of them.

The house was silent. The only sound was the scrape of lawn chairs on the living room tiles as Martha and Beryl sat down. The light came from dozens of candles. Frances sat in her wheelchair. Anzuela and Sasha sat on the floor.

When she sat down and looked around, Sasha realized all the girls' name tags had changed: "Master" for Martha, "Fringe" for Frances, "Zorro" for Anzuela, and "BB" for Beryl.

Master handed a name tag to Sasha that said "Sage."

"These are just the quirky names we use for each other," Master explained. "You're Sage because you are wise with the computer. So from now on, when we're together we call each other by these names. It's kind of like a secret club."

"What is this place?" Sasha asked putting the name tag around her neck. "And where are the other volunteers?"

Master waved her hand around the room. "Oh, this place? My father's in real estate — expensive real estate. Whenever there's an empty house around, he lets us use it for a meeting. Nice, isn't it?"

"And we wanted to talk to you about a particular job," added Zorro. "You know, take the time to fill you in personally. So we didn't invite anyone else. Does that make sense?"

"I guess," Sasha answered. It was a little weird, but kind of exciting too. She definitely wanted to know more about the CREW.

All the girls looked different than they did at school. Unlike Sasha, their clothes were more attention-grabbing than stylish. Master's long hair was on top of her head in a tower of black. Her slashed jeans ended in black cowboy boots. Zorro's shorts were even shorter than Sasha had first realized, and showed off the cheeks of her bum. Fringe looked ten years older than a high school girl. Her white silk shirt was open almost to her navel and it was clear she wasn't wearing a bra. Her black wide-legged pants draped her legs. It was BB's hair and English accent, rather than clothes, that set her apart. Her curly red hair was an aura around her face. Like Sasha had worn earlier in the day, BB was in black jeans and a sweater.

"Let me tell you about our little CREW, Sasha," Master said in her smoky voice. "I know we look different from how we do at school. But that's just our style. At school and with our volunteer gigs, we have to look the part of leaders. We go a little wild when we're alone. So next time, you might want to dress down a bit."

"Sure," Sasha said. She could take a hint. Her new, perfect leather outfit was over the top.

"Now," Master said as she turned to the rest of the girls. "Work before pleasure. What are the jobs on our list?"

BB pulled out her phone and faced the others. "We have three dog-walking jobs. The money we get will go toward the fencing in of the dog park." Her eager smile was rewarded by Master's nod. "And I collected seventy-two dollars from a nice guy I met on the bus. That will go to kids' transportation."

BB pulled her hair up, tying it back with an elastic from her pocket. Then she got up from her chair and handed a wallet to Master, turning her back to Sasha and the others.

That's odd, Sasha thought. Was it BB's hair pulled back? Her jeans? The sight triggered a memory of the scene she witnessed on the bus. Of course she couldn't be sure because she never did see the girl's face, but . . .

Sasha decided to forget it. She did not want to stir up trouble now for no reason.

"Now the job for you, Sage," Master was saying, "is to visit the Garden Seniors' Residence. You will help the old people set up bank accounts on their computers. We've already volunteered there lots of times, reading to the residents, playing games with them, taking them out for walks. But with your talent we can really help them become more independent. That's what they really want."

Sasha asked, "When?"

"Zorro and you will go over there after school on Monday, okay?" Master told her. Sasha nodded. "You'll need police clearance to work with seniors, but we have several forms already signed by the head of the residence. She knows we send volunteers there. As long as it's filled in and sent, and you have a passport and immigration papers, you're good to go."

"I have them," said Sasha.

"Bring them with you on Monday," Zorro added.

"So, Sage," Master drawled. She leaned back into her lawn chair. "What's your story? Other than that you're good with computers."

Sasha felt a bit uneasy being the centre of attention. "You know I come from Russia," she started. "My father is with the government there. My mother and I live in a house in Rosedale. We came so I can learn English." New friends didn't need to know about old friends.

"Whoa, Rosedale," said Fringe. "That's big money." As Zorro nudged her, she added, "But you speak very good English."

"I learned in school. But it's not good enough. My father says it must be perfect. But I like it here, so it's okay."

"That's all the good stuff. What about the bad stuff?" Master peered into Sasha's face. "Isn't your father a minister of justice in Russia? At least that's what I read — that the minister's daughter and wife were making a sudden move to Canada. Would that be you? Why did you really move to Canada, Sasha?"

Where would Master have read that? Sasha knew that the story of the hacking was posted for about a day on a Russian social media site. But it had been quickly taken down. Sasha's alarm at the question must have shown on her face.

"Oh, don't worry, Sage," said Master. "It was probably just fake news. There seems to be a lot of misinformation that comes out of Russia.

"Anyway let's celebrate your new family, the CREW," Master went on. She pulled a bottle of vodka and plastic glasses from her bag. "I figured you'd like vodka, since you're from Russia and all. We all love it." She opened the bottle, poured some of the liquor into each of the glasses, and passed them around. "What do you say in Russia for *cheers,* Sage?"

Chapter 6

A Crack in the CREW

Sasha had never expected that after less than one week at her new school she'd be drinking vodka with a group of girls.

"We say *na zdorovie* to toast," said Sasha. "It means 'To your health.'" And she raised her glass to her new friends.

"Okay," said Master, "Naz drovy or whatever." She threw the shot back. The others followed.

Sasha figured all the girls were about her

age, fifteen or sixteen. Maybe Master was older. And she knew the legal drinking age here was nineteen. But Sasha was used to vodka. Her crowd always drank it. Even so, her father was very strict about drinking outside of family gatherings. Now, with everyone watching, she tossed it down like a pro. Cold and fiery at the same time, it hit her stomach with a thud and spread warmth through her entire body.

Master was already pouring seconds. Worried about what her mother would say if she came home drunk, Sasha stood up. "I have to go. Anzuela . . . uh, Zorro, don't worry. I'll get the bus at the bottom of the street. I'll see you all on Monday at school."

Zorro was on her feet and in front of the door before Sasha could turn around. "Hey," Zorro said. "It's Friday night. You can stay out a little longer." She pulled Sasha back into the room.

"We're just getting started," said Master. She was rolling something in cigarette paper as she walked over to Sasha. "Have you ever smoked this stuff? Here, hold it for a minute. Everyone, get in here." Master called out. She pulled out a phone and took a selfie of the group before Sasha could hide what she knew was weed. "Remember these photos are just for us . . . for fun. What goes on with the CREW stays with the CREW. Right?"

Sasha handed the joint back to Master. She'd tried marijuana at home, but didn't like it because it made her lose control. And Sasha liked control. She figured Master did too. "I prefer vodka," said Sasha. "Maybe I will have another drink."

Sasha's weekend was taken up with family stuff. Her weekly Skype session with her father gave her a chance to brag about her new friends and how they did all this good work. They spoke in English and even her father had trouble keeping up with her.

Saturday night, at another party, this time at the Russian Consulate, her mother insisted she wear her new dress. There, everyone greeted Sasha and her mother like they were royalty. The attention was over the top and Sasha couldn't figure out why. But she was in a good mood, knowing she had her own friends now. She ended up having a pretty good time, especially after the bartender slipped her vodka.

After school on Monday, Sasha met Zorro in the hall and they walked to the seniors' residence. It was clear Zorro knew her way around the place. The girl behind the desk said hello, looked at Sasha's papers, and sent them to the common room. Sasha's grandmother had been in one of these places in Moscow. Although this place was much nicer, the smell of pee and overcooked vegetables still won out over the air freshener.

People were playing cards, talking, watching TV. Some were making conversation or doing puzzles. And some were just staring into space.

Zorro approached someone sitting at a computer. The woman looked up, pleased to see her. "Hi, Grace," said Zorro. "I want to introduce Sasha. She's new to the city from Russia, but she knows a ton of stuff about the computer. She's going to help you set up your bank account online. You'll be able to see how much money you have at any time. You can also transfer money for bills, or send money to your grandchildren. I know you like to do that."

"Oh, that's great," said Grace. "Hello, Sasha. Welcome to Canada. You sit down right here beside me and show me what to do. I already went to my bank with all my identification. Anzuela took me, and stepped out of the room when I was giving personal information. She's so nice, that Anzuela. Now

I have to learn all the bits and pieces on the computer."

Grace was sweet. She reminded Sasha of her grandmother before she'd died. Sasha sat down beside her, and Zorro hung back, but close enough to see and hear.

"Do you have your bank account number?" Sasha asked.

"Here's all the information right here," Grace answered. She held up her ATM card and a piece of paper with her bank name and branch, bank account number, and her PIN number. From behind, Zorro tapped something into her phone.

"No, no, Grace," said Sasha, pushing the paper away. "That is secret information. You should not show that to anyone. It's just for when you use the ATM. What you'll need for the computer is a password."

Sasha opened the bank's website and showed Grace how to log in. "Now for your secret password. Don't tell me, just think of something you will remember every time. It should have some letters and some numbers."

Grace thought for a moment. Then she blurted out: "I have it. Grands-one-two-three for my three grandchildren. How's that?"

Sasha sighed and looked at Zorro. Zorro smiled back before walking away. "I'll be back," she said, texting something on her phone.

Sasha turned back to Grace. "But now I know your password, Grace. You should choose another one."

"No, I like that one. You're a good girl. You're not going to tell anyone, are you?"

"No. It's all right, I guess," said Sasha.

Suddenly, Grace's face darkened. "Yes, a good girl. Not like my second daughter. She never visits or phones. And she tells everyone I need to be put into a more secure home. I'm finished with her. The first thing I'm going to do is to cut her off from my monthly payments."

Sasha was shocked. She didn't want to

hear all this personal stuff. And she and Zorro shouldn't be in the middle of this old lady's personal business. Grace seemed pretty angry with her daughter . . . but was that Sasha's concern?

Sasha knew Zorro heard the password too, and vowed to talk to her about it later. For the moment, all she could do was help Grace set up and open the new online account. For the next hour, Sasha showed Grace how to move money between her accounts, how to pay bills online, and how to send money to someone as a transfer. Grace seemed to understand everything and asked Sasha to come back in a week to see that everything was all right.

Sasha found Zorro outside on her phone. "Do you think it's okay?" Zorro was saying. Then, "Yeah, we're good," she replied and hung up.

Sasha jumped in. "Now we know her password."

Zorro smiled and said, "Oh, it's fine. I'm not going to tell anyone, are you?"

Sasha gave her usual response. "I guess."

Did everyone trust her not to tell Grace's information? Maybe in Canada there were ways to protect your private information that she didn't know of. She'd look it up so she'd be ready if something went wrong.

Chapter 7

Proof of Loyalty

The week passed by quickly. To Sasha's surprise and delight, Jake was very attentive. Even though Sasha hadn't planned on seeing guys right away, he was slowly breaking down her resistance. He met her at her locker at 8:30 every morning. This made her want to get to school early. Her mother assumed the urgency was Sasha's love of school.

On Friday after school, the CREW met in another beautiful home that was empty of furniture.

"Another house for sale?" asked Sasha.

"Oh yeah," BB answered. "It belongs to my aunt. She's got someone getting it ready to sell. She's in Mexico, so I thought it wouldn't hurt to have our meeting here. She won't mind. She's good."

The vodka came out along with a joint, and the party was on. Sasha said no to all of it.

"So, Sashh-shha," said Master.

After a couple of shots and most of a joint, Master was losing it. The others laughed at the way she slurred Sasha's name.

"What do you want to get out of being a CREW member?" Master asked. "We all have our reasons for belonging. What's yours?" Master sat up straight and tried to focus.

Sasha thought for a moment. How much should she tell them? "I like the idea of helping others," she said carefully. "Not only for me but because my parents will see that I'm fitting into the 'right' crowd. But mostly I really want friends. Real friends."

Sitting next to her on the floor, BB hugged Sasha.

"My friends at home were . . ." Sasha went on. "Well, let's just say what Master found online about us coming to Canada is true. I got into some trouble at home. My so-called friends used my skills to get what they wanted. They didn't really care about me." Sasha was silent for a moment. "I don't want to talk about it. I really want the CREW to be a new beginning."

"We want that too," said Master. "And as you get to know the CREW better, you'll understand that everyone has some skin in the game." She turned to Fringe. "Isn't that right? I think it means we have to put in something to get something out."

Through her laughter, Fringe managed, "I have absolutely no idea what you're saying, Master. It sounds really stupid."

BB turned to Sasha. "You know, we are all, like, sort of orphans here. And not everybody in school likes to hook up with an orphan. When I came from England I felt so alone and embarrassed about my accent. I needed extra tutoring because I was behind in a lot of subjects and that made me feel stupid. Then the CREW took me in and now my confidence is a lot higher. Ta da!" She threw her hands in the air. "Whatever we do," she added, "we do for each other."

"Listen," BB continued, "Master grew up in foster care. Home after home, dealing with abuse. Even time on the streets. She's pretty tough, I know." She looked to Master to make sure she wasn't going too far. Master responded with a tight smile. "But she is the smartest person I know. And if it weren't for Master, I don't think I'd have any friends at all."

Fringe wheeled over. "Do you think you have it that bad, Sage? You're in the best country in the world, in a terrific house, with lots of money. Some of us have been on the outside all our lives. Chairs like this," she said, pointing down, "have been part of my life since I was five years old. I barely survived a car accident."

Fringe dropped her head so BB carried on Fringe's story. "Fringe was wrecked and had no time for friends with all her therapy. Master met her at a disadvantaged children's camp where Master was working in the kitchen. They became friends. Now look at Fringe. Beautiful and confident."

Stunned as well as ashamed, Sasha looked at Zorro for her story.

"Me too," said Zorro. "Finding friends wasn't easy for me, you know. I've been teased and bullied all my life because I'm so small."

"But that's not her fault," Master butted in. "Zorro has a condition that gets in the way of her growth hormones. But here with the CREW, she can show the strength she has, not in spite of, but because of her condition. She charms everyone."

"We all have a special bond," BB continued. "We've been together since grade seven and we look out for each other. Our home-lives are second to the CREW. My parents are okay, but don't realize how much loyalty I owe my friends. So we pledge never to tell our parents what we're up to."

Zorro's baby face lit up. "And we have fun, don't we girls? And we do help out real causes all the time. We get money from people who don't deserve what they have and we give to charities we like. We keep just a little for our efforts. That's it."

Sasha's mind was a rollercoaster, rumbling up with pity and crashing down with affection. The words had touched her. They made her think about her own privilege. Her "fun" in Moscow was just that, fun. But the CREW's activities came out of love for each other while they gave the finger to the jerks in the world. And they did good things.

Sasha's father had told her she needed to

take responsibility for her actions. She was ready to do that. She wanted to be different here and the CREW was giving her that chance. She could help others and still belong. She remembered a story her parents read her when she was little. It was the Russian translation of Robin Hood, about an English bandit who took from the rich and gave to the poor. She loved that story. Maybe now she could live it.

Master got up and stood in front of Sasha. "We really want you as part of our group. You're talented and smart. And you're going to need good friends here. There are a lot of kids in this school who think that anyone from another country or who grew up in another situation is shit. We don't want that to be you, because that was us."

Sasha's need to belong pushed her. "I want to be part of the CREW," she said. "I really do."

There were cheers all around and almost a smile from Master.

Master went on. "So we think you should start by giving us the password for old Grace's account. Oh and I guess we'll need the account number and the bank too." She smirked as the others watched for Sasha's reaction.

"What?" Sasha was stunned. After their confessions about going after only bad guys, Sasha wasn't sure she'd heard right. Grace wasn't a bad guy. "You know I can't tell you that. I shouldn't even know it."

"Oh, come on. It's not like we'll make it public knowledge. But we're moving on some other things and we need to show a bank account as credentials. That's it." The words were reasonable, but Master's dark eyes seemed to mock Sasha. Then Master smiled and went back to her chair.

From leader to bully and back again. Master reminded Sasha of her father. He could be really scary one minute and a doting father the next. Sasha's way to handle him was to go along and be humble. Maybe that would work with Master too.

"I understand," Sasha's voice quavered. "But doesn't Zorro know it? She was there too."

"This is a test Sasha. Yes, Zorro gave it to us, but we want you to show us your loyalty. You show us you are loyal to us and you are one step further to becoming true CREW."

It suddenly hit Sasha. She could go to prison for getting involved in Grace's account. But in the end, she figured she had the computer skills to erase her part in the deception if she needed to. She checked the card in her bag and told the CREW Grace's account number and password. She'd check Grace's account on Monday. It would probably be okay.

Chapter 8

The True CREW

On Monday, Sasha went straight to the seniors'
residence when she got out of school. She
found Grace disturbed and confused.

"I'm sure I did everything right," Grace
said. Sasha could see that tears were ready to
spill down her cheeks. "But it looks like there's
money missing. It must be my fault. Nobody
else has touched this computer all week."

Sasha confirmed that money had been
transferred to something called Seniors' Advice.

When Sasha asked if Grace knew of any organization she supported or that might be part of the residence, Grace shook her head.

"Never heard of it," Grace said. "But it could be right. I've given money to a lot of causes in the past. What should I do?"

"Don't worry for now," Sasha told her. "I'll check with your bank. It could all be a big mistake." She tried to make her voice positive, but she suspected the CREW's meddling was behind it.

Another emergency waited for Sasha at home. Her mother was Skyping with her father and she heard her father say, "She needs to come home if she doesn't obey. Her clothes, her new friends you do not know. What is going on?"

Before her mother could answer, Sasha slipped in next to her on the couch and said brightly, "Hi, Papa. What's going on?" Luckily she was dressed conservatively for her visit to the seniors' home. Her hair was in a ponytail and she was wearing a long-sleeved red shirt with black jeans.

"Ah, *kotyonok moya*," her father greeted her.

"Papa, I'm too old to be called your little kitten. I'm a big cat now."

Her father laughed and Sasha went on. "I just came back from helping an old lady at a seniors' home. It's my volunteer work here." She stole a look at her mother, who squinted back at her.

"Wonderful," said her father. "We have taught you well. And you look lovely. Your mother said your clothes were too sexy."

"Oh, that," said Sasha. "I bought a couple of shorter skirts because everyone wears them here. I'm not nearly as daring as some of them. And I don't want to be. I want you and Mother to be proud of me."

"Oh *kotyonok*, you seem just fine to me. But . . ." he shook his finger, "if you give your mother grief, I will have you home in one day. You know that."

"Yes, Papa. Here's Mother. I have homework to do." With another quick look at her mother's disapproving face, Sasha raced upstairs. Her mother would be up soon enough to "discuss."

As soon as she was in her room, Sasha checked into Grace's account. It was true. Five hundred dollars had been transferred to Seniors' Advice. When Sasha tried to figure out what Seniors' Advice was, she could find no address or website. All she could find was that it was a non-profit organization. Did that mean a charity? Maybe a charity didn't go by the same rules as other places.

Sasha suspected the CREW, but she had to make absolutely sure. She wasn't going to panic yet. The CREW knew the rules a lot better than she did. Sasha promised herself that she would be more watchful when she was with them. She remembered the addresses of the two houses she'd been in and searched them. Up came information that both were for sale or just sold. That fit their stories about why there wasn't much furniture. Still, she'd watch for any clues that the CREW wasn't supposed to be there.

∗∗∗

At school the next day, Sasha deliberately bumped into Zorro walking down the hall. "I'm kind of worried that something is going on," she said. "Five hundred dollars was transferred from Grace's account to something called Seniors' Advice."

Zorro kept walking and whispered. "Never mind that right now. Come to the library after last class for our next meeting."

Sasha's thoughts throughout the day shifted between Grace's money and the meeting tonight. In Moscow, she and her friends invaded people's privacy. But they never really crossed the line — until the prime minister's affair. Sasha was no angel, that's for sure. But she had promised her father to stay on the right path. She really did want to do that.

On her way to the meeting, Sasha saw her mother walking into the school office. She hurried over to find her mother and Master face to face in front of the secretary's desk — a picture of opposites, and it wasn't just their ages. Her mother wore a fine yellow wool suit over a white silk blouse. Master wore her usual faded blazer, uneven skirt, and held some papers, which she quickly dropped on the secretary's desk.

"Mother, what are you doing here?" Sasha asked.

In Russian, her mother said: "Just checking on my girl. I want to talk to the principal about how you are doing. You don't need to come in with me."

Master looked at Sasha and mouthed: "Introduce me."

"Uh, Mother, this is my friend Mast . . .

uh, Martha. She's with that group I told you about."

"I'm the head of that group, Mrs. Asinov. I really appreciate how helpful Sasha's been at the seniors' home. You should be very proud of her."

Frowning slightly, Sasha's mother looked Master up and down. She said, "How do you do?" then turned away, ignoring Master like she was an annoying mosquito. In Russian, she said to Sasha, "I'll see you at home later." She waltzed into the principal's office.

Master looked at Sasha, nodding slowly. Then she said, "We'd better get to the meeting."

Sasha agreed. She needed to see what they had to say about Grace's account. If it were part of a test or a joke, she'd find out. Then, she'd be accepted. But after her mother's snub of Master, she wasn't sure it would go that well.

Master ushered Sasha into a side room in the library, then closed and locked the door. The CREW would not be disturbed.

Sasha waited for Master to say something about her mother. But Master launched into a report on how much money they had made that month.

"Fringe arranged one hundred dollars a month from her church's foundation. That gives socks to the homeless. And Zorro and Sage together brought in five hundred dollars for Seniors' Advice, our blog on ways to help seniors. I have five hundred dollars from the lottery we put on for the teachers on their PA day. Someone won a trip to Jamaica and we pocketed five hundred dollars for our personal causes."

Sasha's mind raced. Seniors' Advice? Five hundred dollars? What was going on? Was that the money that came out of Grace's account? She had helped set up Grace's account. She had given the CREW the account and password. Grace said $500 was missing. And now $500 showed up connected to Seniors' Advice.

Sasha was starting to worry that the CREW was not what it appeared to be. She liked these girls. Well, Master was hard to like. But she was smart, as BB said. If they were out to get innocent people, though, she didn't want to be here.

Big applause from the CREW cut into her thoughts. Master was saying, "That's eleven hundred dollars this week. Each of us gets a cut." She handed a crisp one hundred dollar bill to each CREW member. "The rest goes in the pot. And here's more good news. I got us all tickets to the Grisly Grizzlies at the Danforth Music Hall on Saturday. It's not all work and no play with the CREW."

Another gift? Or a bribe?

"Sage, this is cool, right?" Master stood in front of Sasha, holding out her one hundred dollar bill. When Sasha didn't move to take it, her smile turned to a scowl. "I said, isn't this great?"

"I guess," Sasha's usual response triggered a new response from Master. Sasha had seen Master's sarcasm, greed, and manipulation. Now she saw fury.

"You guess? You *guess*?" Master's voice rose. "Why is that always your only response?" Master stomped to the front of the room and ripped down the CREW sign that said Confident, Remarkable, Excellent, Welcoming.

Fringe wheeled over: "Not yet, Master. She's not ready."

But Master just ignored Fringe. She turned the poster around and held it up in Sasha's face.

On the back, the poster read:

The CREW

Con

Rip-off

Exploit

Weaken

Chapter 9

Trapped

Sasha covered her eyes. This was no joke or test. This was the real thing.

Master pulled Sasha's hands down and held them, forcing her to look at the poster. Her fingers dug into Sasha's wrists. Master's mouth twitched as if it were hard to get the words out. Finally, she spoke in a voice so low it was almost a whisper. "Don't you see this, Sage? This is who we are. Your mother might not approve. But this is it."

Master turned to face the rest of the girls. "Oh, by the way," she said in a nasty voice. "I met Sasha's mother. She's high-class Russian all right. The clothes, the jewellery, the snobby attitude, the very bad accent. She wouldn't even speak to me."

Fringe and Zorro looked on eagerly, waiting for Sasha's reaction. Only BB spoke up. "Hey, Master," she said. "Go a little easy, okay? She's new at this."

Master threw her hands up in the air and walked out of the room.

"Remember what I told you, Sasha," said BB. "About all of us. We need each other. And if Master gets mad at the world and how it puts us down, well, she has a right."

Zorro's baby voice said, "She's like a mother to us, Sasha. Or at least a guardian angel."

"We all have flaws —" started Fringe.

"And Master's is her temper," finished BB.

Master came back and bumped BB out of the way. She stood in front of Sasha. Through clenched teeth, she said, "I'm sorry I got so upset, Sasha. We really want you as part of our group. You're talented and smart. And you're going to need good friends here."

"I want to be part of the CREW," Sasha said. Even if she didn't, she had to be careful here. "It's just . . ." Before she could finish, she saw Master's eyes narrow.

Sasha pushed on. "It's just . . ." Sasha took a deep breath. "I don't know why we need to steal from Grace. Maybe from the government or big business, or really bad people. "

Sasha could see that Master was ready to explode again. Zorro answered quickly, "Because Grace is a bitch who wants to cut her children out of her will. She's lucky to have children."

"Yes, but she's just an old lady. And what about the man on the bus? I saw BB take the wallet with the seventy-two dollars. What was wrong with him?"

BB responded. "You didn't tell us you were watching that day. Sneaky, Sasha. Didn't you see him leaning into me so he could feel my boobs? Didn't you notice how he was checking my ass? He's a dirty old man."

Sasha knew she had to be careful. "It's just that I think I can be much more helpful to the CREW in other ways. I can do a lot on the computer. In Moscow, I was known for getting information from secure sites. I can do that here too. We don't have to target innocent people.

"Besides," Sasha went on. An image of her grandmother popped into Sasha's mind every time she thought of Grace. "I didn't know I should be careful with Grace. I left myself open to being caught. The woman at the front desk knows Zorro came in with me that day, so she could be in trouble too." Sasha hadn't been that careless, but she didn't want to be part of stealing from Grace.

Zorro turned to Master. "She's right, Master. Think about letting Grace go. Sage can do much more on the next job to make up for it."

Master had been leaning against the wall, staring at Sasha as she spoke. But now she sauntered back to where Sasha was sitting. Then she leaned down and hugged Sasha. The rest of the CREW crowded around into a group hug.

Sasha was surprised and touched. In Moscow she was never sure if her friends liked her for herself or because of her father's position and money. But these girls were willing to let a sure source of money go because Sasha asked. Wasn't this proof that the CREW really were her friends?

"I think your father would approve of our actions," added Master.

She doubted he would approve. But at least she wouldn't be stealing from old women. Sasha was ready to take on some bad guys. She stood up. "Yes. BFFs!" she shouted, then "Is that how you say it?"

Everyone laughed.

"But here's the thing," said Master. "Sasha, we all have something on each other to ensure our loyalty to one another. So if anyone tries to turn on the others, something will happen. You know . . . police action, expulsion from school, or . . ." looking at Sasha, "deportation. So we all have to work hard to stay together.

"In your case, Sasha," she went on, "our insurance is that you took part in getting Grace's account numbers." She pulled out her phone and showed Sasha the picture Zorro took of Grace showing Sasha her private information. Sasha gasped. "And even though we will give the money back," Master said, "this could seriously damage your reputation. And so could this." She showed the selfie of Sasha holding the joint.

There was no confusion over those threats. Sasha now was absolutely sure that Master and the CREW would blackmail her to keep her quiet. If they had the pictures, what else did they have? Sasha decided she would be extra careful about showing herself. From now on, no cameras and no exposure. If they wouldn't protect her, she had to protect herself.

Master pinned the poster back up with the good side showing. "Now for today's assignment," she continued. "I have about fifty contact numbers. You don't need to know how I got them. All the numbers are of men who have a reputation for going after young girls."

Sasha didn't like the sound of this.

Fringe piped up. "I see you squirming, Sasha. But you don't have to have sex with them."

Sasha let her breath out.

"No, just pretend you want to," Master said. "Anyway, this represents an opportunity but I'm not sure how to exploit it. That's where you come in, Sasha. How do we catch these guys? Maybe with these pictures?"

Master showed Sasha a tablet with a series of photographs of herself and Fringe from the waist up. Both were wearing skimpy bras and see-through camis. Full, slightly open lips and eyes closed, their expressions said they were in the middle of sex. As the pictures were going around, Master stared at Sasha for an answer.

This was definitely a bigger target than Grace's account. And these guys were perverts going after young girls. Sasha nodded. "We could lure them to do more and pay for it. We send suggestive pictures of the CREW to these guys with lines like, 'Tonight, just you and me.' That gets them interested. We say we'll show more skin if they send us their pictures with them wearing as little as possible. Their faces should show they are thinking of us so we can be thinking of them."

"Can you do that, Sasha?" Master was almost drooling. "They do illegal things all the time, you know. They search the web for sites with underage girls so they can jerk off without their wives knowing. They have to pay for that."

"I think so," Sasha replied. "I can set up a website with a firewall so they won't be able to trace us. When they send their pictures to us, I'll combine their pictures with the CREW's pictures in sexy poses and send them back."

Fringe interrupted. "And we get them to pay — five hundred dollars a shot — to keep the pictures from their wives and bosses."

Master jumped in. "Yes, five hundred a shot. Now we're talking."

"Hey," said Sasha, "I thought we would just teach them a lesson. We don't have to go to blackmail. Maybe one or two of the worst ones, but . . ."

Master turned to her and smirked. "You know, Sage, you're like one of those Russian dolls. A smaller and smaller doll is revealed every time you open one up. You're with us, but when we open you up, you're a doll who questions everything. We open that one up and you desperately want to belong. Then we open the last one up and you are this little shivering doll at the bottom."

Then, suddenly serious, Master asked Sasha, "The question is, can you do this?"

Chapter 10

Crime for Good

Sasha could do it. She could lure the men online and protect the CREW. But she would have to be careful to get rid of any evidence quickly. "Blackmail is illegal. You know, I'll be the one who'll be in trouble if it goes wrong. If they're computer-smart, they could tell who is trying to communicate with them from my IP address. And if I'm caught, the police can force me to turn over photos of us and the information on these men."

"Oh, shit," said Master. "Are you going to whine about every idea we have? We don't need to know all the technical details."

Before another blow-up, BB interrupted. "Sage, these guys are creeps. They are breaking a major law. So we break a minor law to get them. And we get to send the money to a shelter for abused girls."

Sasha's mind turned to her father's world of corruption and greed. She thought about her own petty crime at home. Maybe she was really a bad seed. Why else would she see the justice in this?

"You're right," Sasha agreed. Scamming guys who prey on young girls was the kind of thing she could justify. But remembering her own rule just a few minutes ago, she said, "But one thing." Master got ready to pounce, but Sasha went on. "I will do all the computer work and combine the photos. But I won't appear in any pictures. And we have one week to do as much as we can. But then, I'm cutting it off. Even though I'm good, the longer I'm exposed, the more chance there is that someone will find me out."

Sasha could see Master planning a tough comeback. But she heard Fringe's voice from behind. "I agree. Sasha needs to concentrate on the computer and communications. If she's uncomfortable with the other part, it will only distract her."

"Okay," Master relented. "But, Zorro, as her control, you better keep her on track."

"No problem, right, Sage? When do we start?"

Master already had her jacket on and was gathering up her books. "Friday night. I'll email the names this week and we'll finalize then."

Right, thought Sasha, *in another empty house for sale.*

Before she left, Master called everyone together into another group hug. Whatever happened, Sasha thought, she had a group of friends. And life in Canada sure wasn't dull.

They all went their separate ways. BB headed to the subway a block away. Zorro got into her smart car. And Master got on a motorcycle with a very hot guy. Fringe had a Wheel-Trans van pick her up and asked Sasha if she wanted a ride.

"I'll get off first and they'll take you home, okay? You can be my attendant, so it's part of the service."

"Sure. Great. And thanks for standing up for me with Master back there. I really don't want to get into the sex trade."

"No problem," said Fringe. "I find it kind of fun. I always wonder what they'd think if they could see the whole me. I know there are dudes who are into that."

When they got to Fringe's home, she asked Sasha, "Hey, do you want to come in? We could watch Netflix. My parents are working until early morning." Her usual confidence was replaced by a longing in her voice that Sasha had never heard before.

"I can't, sorry," said Sasha. "My mom is waiting for me. And by the way, Mother is not as bad as Master made her out. She is a snob, but she's not very confident here on her own, so she plays the role of a rich lady in control."

"It doesn't matter. My place isn't much to come into," Fringe said as the driver helped her out of the truck. Without saying goodbye, she wheeled herself to the front door of an apartment that had an assisted living sign. A woman who looked old enough to be Fringe's grandmother stood waiting.

That night, Sasha's racing heart wouldn't let her sleep. She thought about the meeting and all the CREW members. Seeing how Fringe lived made her depressed. She thought about how the CREW got their money and what they did with it. And how she had basically agreed to blackmail people. But those guys were perverts. Now maybe they'd think twice before surfing for children.

Life was really different for Sasha these days. But the longer she stayed in Canada, the less she wanted to go back to Moscow. School was good and she was learning English very quickly. She had new clothes that were so much better than at home. Her mother was even giving her more freedom to go out with her friends. And with her CREW money, she would be able to go to concerts, to the mall, to the gym — wherever — without nagging her mom for money.

No way she wanted to lose all that.

And Jake. She didn't encourage Jake. But she loved that he looked for her all the time. She felt a thrill run through her every time he stopped her in the halls to talk.

On Friday, at the usual 8:30 meet at her locker, Jake said, "So you're one of the CREW now? People say they do good things. But Martha is a little creepy. She's always making a point of talking or standing next to me in a group. What's the deal with her, anyway?"

Before Sasha could answer, Jake leaned in and kissed her. Sasha pulled back quickly.

"What, you don't want to?" said Jake. He leaned in again. "Or did I just surprise you?"

Quickly, Sasha looked around to see who was watching. She didn't need the principal calling her mother about her loose behaviour in the halls. But there was Jake, inches away. Sasha leaned in too. "The second part," she said. Her lips were ready for him this time.

The crash of a nearby locker door pulled them apart. Then they were looking into a pair of fierce, black, and very angry eyes. Sasha could see right away that this was not Martha. This was Master. She looked older and tougher. Her dark-lined eyes and black-red lipstick set off her new stringy haircut.

Bumping Sasha out of the way, the girl pushed herself next to Jake. "Oh, sorry. Are you okay, Jake?" Her sweet voice and smile did not match her look.

Jake moved around her to stand next to Sasha again. "What the hell are you doing, Martha? And what are you wearing?"

Only then did Sasha notice Master wasn't wearing her usual school uniform. Her ripped black mini and striped leggings showed off scrawny hips and legs. "You look like one of those zombies on TV," laughed Jake. "What do you think Sasha?"

Sasha knew Master better than Jake. She knew the head of the CREW did not accept insults without a comeback.

Jake was still going on. "You don't scare me, Martha. Or whoever you are today. Come on Sasha, I'll walk you to class."

Sasha caught Master's glare. "Uh, I really have to see the secretary first," Sasha said. "Something about how long I'm in the country.

I'll, um, see you later." And she hurried away from both Jake and Master.

"See you tonight at the meeting, Sasha," Master called out.

Sasha realized that Master always got the last word.

Chapter 11

I Own You

That night at the meeting Master was quiet. Sasha felt her silence was even more disturbing than her angry rants.

The leadership role was left to Fringe, who explained how they would catch perverts online from photos that Sasha would set up. "Then . . ." she finished up, "we ask for the money. We get what we can in one week and close it down. And everything disappears. Right, Sasha?"

Sasha nodded. But she was checking an Instagram link that had just been sent to her. On her screen was a cartoon showing a heart with an arrow through it. At the end of the arrow was a stick figure with long blond hair hanging from a rope. It was a clear threat.

Sasha dropped her phone and ran out of the room. As she fled, she heard Master's voice saying, "Oh, come on, Sage. It's only a joke. Can't you take a joke? BB, go after her. She's going to have to learn to suck it up."

On the way out of the room, BB picked up Sasha's phone. She looked at Master and shook her head. Then she went to find Sasha in the bathroom.

"Look, Sasha," said BB. "It's just Master and her jokes. She doesn't mean anything by it."

"Why does she do those things?" asked Sasha. "She's out to get me, I know it. I like you other girls. But this is getting to be too much."

BB sighed. "Hey, just go along for now. Maybe you could tone it down with Jake? At least when she's around. She's just jealous, but she'll get over it." BB pulled tissues off the counter and handed them to Sasha. "Just remember, we are doing some good. So have some fun with it. We do have fun with the CREW, don't we?"

Determined not to be put down by Master, Sasha walked back to the room with her head high. She thumped down on the couch. She looked up, straight into Master's smirk.

As Fringe talked about timing for getting pictures taken, Sasha continued to glare at Master. Then Sasha said, "Listen, I want to stop these guys as much as you do. And I can do that. But we don't have to fight. Just to be clear, I will set up the photos. But if you want my computer skills, you have to keep me out of the public eye." She folded her arms.

Master turned toward Sasha. "What you don't understand is that I own you, Sage.

Maybe Sage wasn't the right name. You're not being so wise. Maybe your name should be Sissy. Do you know what a sissy is, girl? It's someone who is afraid of everything. And who can't be relied upon to do what she says she'll do.

"You chose us, Sissy," Master went on. "And now you're one of us. If you don't go along with our plan, I will make sure you regret it. Like, your mother will get a note that says her daughter stole from a certain old lady. And I'll include a picture to prove it. Or Jake will be questioned by immigration officials about a friend of his they suspect of fraud."

Sasha felt her bravery cracking under Master's threats. Her only friend was BB. When Sasha looked at her, BB shook her head slightly, telling Sasha not to react.

"Okay," Sasha said lightly. "We don't have to fight."

"See, that was easy," said Master. "But come on, at least one more vodka in friendship.

Here, I'll get it." She took Sasha's glass to the counter. Sasha walked up behind her, just in time to see Master holding a couple of pills over Sasha's drink.

"What are you doing?" Sasha shouted. She grabbed the glass away from Master, who simply smiled.

"Just having a little fun," said Master. "You should try this stuff. It'll loosen you up."

Sasha slammed the glass down on the counter, spilling the vodka, and then gathered up her things. For once, she had the last word. "Na zdorovie!"

***

Her mother and father were Skyping when Sasha got home.

"We'll have to get a bigger house if that happens," she heard her mother say.

If what happens? Sasha wondered. She slipped upstairs, thinking that she had a lot of other things to worry about: her school, the CREW, the old woman's computer. Jake. She didn't have time for her parents' mystery.

✳✳✳

For the next two weeks, Sasha concentrated on the Internet porn scam. When Jake asked why she couldn't see him after school, her excuse was that she was busy with a fundraiser her mother was planning. She told him she was expected to coordinate all the invitations and responses.

But Sasha still saw Jake at school, where they were becoming bolder in front of people. They held hands in the halls. They went to lunch together at the popular café on the corner. They kissed goodbye at the end of the day. A couple of times, they saw Master lurking nearby. It just made them more open with their feelings. They figured Master would back off if she understood they were really together.

At night and on weekends, the CREW posed for Sasha's camera without showing their faces. Fringe was shot from the waist up. Her breasts were very visible in a see-through tank and her face was out of focus. BB was shown from the back in a onesie that exposed her ass. Pretty Zorro, dressed in a very short, frilly dress, sucked her thumb, her hand covering her face. Sasha had no doubt she'd attract anybody looking for an eight year old.

In keeping with her image of Master, their leader posed in a net body suit with nothing underneath. Her face was covered with a net hood and she held a whip.

At one point, Sasha caught Zorro taking pictures of her as the photographer of porn. Sasha just stopped dead. "I'm out of here if that keeps up," she warned. Master took Zorro's phone away and showed Sasha how she was deleting everything Zorro just took.

When the photos of the girls were ready, Sasha sent them to the men. They were attached to a message that Master had prepared, asking them to send their own sexy pictures back.

The men responded eagerly. But what they received in return were photos of themselves with half-naked girls — and a message demanding money. The answers came back right away. Some begged for mercy. Some threatened to call the police. But most sent the money — an e-transfer to a numbered account. There were a few who vowed that their own hackers would catch the person behind this. But Sasha was pretty sure her methods were too good to track.

Chapter 12

Or Else

Master ordered a CREW meeting on a Saturday afternoon. They all met in Master's downtown apartment. This time there was no concierge and no fancy front lobby. Sasha pressed the code and was buzzed up. Everyone was there. Master sat in a large, worn corduroy armchair like it was a throne. She was smiling and waving a shot of vodka. A small, scraggly dog sat on her lap.

So this is the Master's den, thought Sasha.

It was clear that Master's confidence didn't come from privilege. BB had said Master's life wasn't easy, and this confirmed it. The furniture and the carpet were clean but showed years of wear. The kitchen, though spotless, was dingy and full of decades-old appliances.

"Help yourselves to the juice," Master said, pointing to a bottle in a bucket of ice. Zorro handed Sasha a shot of vodka.

"Are your parents here?" Sasha asked. She was feeling a little sorry for Master, and it must have shown in her voice. "Don't be sad for me, little Russian doll," said Master. "This is my place, my very own. As soon as I turned eighteen in January, I got this place of my own. It may not be fancy. But it is all mine." She motioned at the dog. "And Munchy here is my best friend. Except for the CREW, of course. Now, let's get started. Fringe?"

"Okay," reported Fringe. "This week nine thousand dollars were deposited from eighteen bad boys. As we agreed, the whole thing will now be shut down. Sasha, you close off any connection to them. So this is a celebration! Let's party."

More vodka was poured and joints were pulled out. This time, Sasha had brought some Russian vodka as a show of goodwill — and to make sure the vodka was okay.

Finally, when everyone was ready to leave, Master said, "Sage, I think we've kind of gotten off track. I need to say one thing."

Sasha was glad Master made a move first. In her friendliest tone she said, "I agree. It's best if we work together."

"We can work together just fine, as soon as you tell Jake you're through with him. Tell him tonight. I don't want an argument, just split up." Then she turned to the CREW. "We'll meet again tomorrow night, here at seven. Oh, and Sasha. I'll be watching you."

Where was the undying sisterhood? What about Sasha's work and the money it brought in? Sasha's surprise swiftly changed to anger.

"I don't think that's for you to say." She was angry, but she spoke quietly. "Unless Jake tells me he's out."

The rest of the CREW watched the contest. Their eyes switched from Master to Sasha. Sasha even saw a little smile on Fringe's face. Was that support or was she just enjoying the show?

For once, there was no pushback. Master just shrugged as Sasha led the way out, with the others close behind. Sasha pushed the button for the elevator. Then she pushed again and again until her finger stung. BB put her hand on Sasha's shoulder. "Take it easy." Finally, the elevator came.

Out on the street, Sasha walked to the nearest corner and grabbed a cab. She couldn't stand the thought of a long bus ride or the CREW's recap of the meeting.

In the cab she couldn't sit still. The tension felt like little needles sticking into her body.

Every time she thought of Master's words, she almost screamed.

"Are you okay, Miss?" asked the driver. "You look pretty shaken up. Can I do anything?"

"Thank you," she said. "I'll be okay."

The driver continued. "It's just that I have a daughter about your age and she got into drugs last year. It's taken the whole year to go off of them. I hope you're not doing that."

Sasha laughed. "It's not drugs, for sure." *It's much, much worse*, she thought.

As she got out of the cab, Sasha could see someone sitting on the steps of her house. Sasha's heart raced as Jake stood up and walked toward her. All her anger and defiance was gone. Sobs came from the bottom of her belly.

Jake held her tight and told her it was going to be all right. And for a minute she believed him. Then a text came in: *I told you I'd be watching you. Tell him. Now!*

Sasha pulled Jake through the door. "I

can't be seen with you right now," she said. She curled up in the corner of the couch like a scared puppy. Jake sat beside her and tried to put his arm around her. She shook it off and said, "I think I've gotten myself into big trouble. And I don't want you to be part of it." Then she broke down in tears.

By the time the front door opened, Sasha had cried herself calm. She'd just decided to tell Jake the whole thing when her mother walked in. "Well, this is pretty," Sasha's mother said. "Who are you, young man?"

Jake rushed to stand up. Sasha stayed where she was. She was too tired to play her mother's games.

"This is Jake, Mother. He's my boyfriend."

Both Jake and her mother were at a loss for words.

"I had a bad day and asked Jake to come over," Sasha lied. "But he has to go now. Right, Jake?"

Jake smiled and pulled his stuff together.

"Glad you're feeling better, Sasha. Nice to meet you, Mrs. Asinov." And out he went, leaving Sasha smiling and her mother with her mouth open.

"I'm going to do my homework, Mother," said Sasha, heading for her room. "I have a test tomorrow, so please don't come up."

"Wait a minute. How do you know that boy? What about his family? I'm calling your father," her mother rattled on.

"You do what you have to do," answered Sasha.

Sasha lay down and thought of Jake. Her boyfriend? Where did that come from? But Jake seemed okay with it. She couldn't wait to see him at school tomorrow. And if she did, what would Master do?

The next morning Sasha's mother was waiting for her in the kitchen. All she got out was "I talked to your father —"

Sasha grabbed a banana and left her with, "We'll talk tonight, Mother."

At school she went straight to her locker. Jake was waiting there.

"Oh, shit," he said. "Did you get into trouble?"

"No, I don't think so. Mother said she told my father. But I don't think she did. I would have heard from him. Besides, she likes it too much here to ruin it."

Jake took her hand. "More importantly, am I your boyfriend?"

"I think you are," she answered.

Before she completely lost herself in his eyes, her phone buzzed. She had an email. It said: *Do you think I can't see you?* Then it showed a scanned bank statement from a bank in the US. The account was in the name of Sasha Asinov. There were deposits made on two dates. Beside each deposit the source had been handwritten: *$500 — Grace's transfer to Seniors' Advice*, and *$9,000 — porn photography and blackmail of eighteen men.*

These words were followed by: *And I have more.* There was a short video of Sasha taking the porn shots of the CREW. The other girls' faces had been blanked out. But Sasha's was very clear.

A text followed: *I can show the world who you really are. LEAVE HIM ALONE! OR ELSE!*

Sasha texted back: *I know who you are, Martha or Master. Do you think this will stop me from seeing Jake? You're wrong!*

Whatever happened, she wasn't giving in and she wasn't giving up.

After school, she told Jake she was sick and had to go home. Her head was pounding. Her fluttering stomach threatened to bring up the banana, which was the only thing she had eaten all day. Her hands shook. All this because of one bully. But, Sasha realized, Master was a bully who needed her.

Chapter 13

Power Play

When Sasha got home, her mother was out, as usual. So Sasha had the house to herself. A bath and trash TV was what she needed. She had to have all her strength for the CREW meeting that night.

BB called, saying she'd received word that they were meeting at another apartment. She and Sasha planned to meet at the subway exit so they could walk to the address together.

As soon as Sasha got there, BB started

talking. She said that Master was completely obsessed with Sasha and Jake's thing.

"Everybody but you has been getting texts from her, calling you a traitor and pushing us toward accusing you of serious crimes. She's not really leading anymore. Zorro and Fringe are fighting over who should be the next leader. I want out. I think you do too."

"But," said Sasha, "what if we get Master out and someone else takes over? We'll be right back where we started. They have the evidence of our crimes. It would just get worse and worse. How do we defend ourselves?"

"What about you as our new leader?" asked BB.

Sasha shook her head. Sasha knew that Master's time had to come to an end. She also knew she was the one to make it happen. But take over? No thanks.

When they reached the lobby of a new luxury apartment, BB rang the buzzer code again and again. They were about to leave when the main door buzzed open. The guy at the desk was dealing with the delivery of several packages. The girls slipped by unnoticed. They took the elevator up to the fifteenth floor.

As they stepped off the elevator, they heard loud voices. Zorro opened an apartment door and stuck her head out, motioning for them to come quickly. They hadn't even stepped in when they heard something big and heavy crashing to the floor.

They found Fringe lying on the floor, her wheelchair tipped over. A glass-fronted bookcase lay in pieces all around her.

BB ran to her. "Fringe, are you all right? What happened? Fringe? Talk to me."

Finally, Fringe moved. "I'm fine," she groaned. "Just get me back into my chair." Sasha and BB each took an arm and lifted her, carefully avoiding the shards of glass to one side of her. When she was settled, she looked at Zorro. "Well?" said Fringe, glaring at Zorro.

"Don't 'well' me," cut in Zorro. "You did this to get attention. You got it. Now what are we going to do about this mess? The owners will be back tonight and poor little Fringe is too weak to clean it up by herself. Or replace the cabinet."

"Where's Master?" interrupted Sasha in a quiet voice.

Zorro turned to her like she was seeing her for the first time. "Master doesn't need to know any of this," said Zorro. "Master isn't interested in us since you joined our CREW. She's only interested in you and Jake. So," she said, looking up at Sasha, "I'm taking over. It's logical, isn't it? I'm the smartest. I get by the best with my little girl act. And," she said, looking back at Fringe, "I can get into most places on my own two feet."

Fringe's beautiful face had turned into a mask. "You will regret that, Zorro," she said. "You're on your own with the cabinet and how to explain it to Master. I'll just tell her you're trying to take over." She pushed herself over to the door.

"Wait," said BB. "We've got to do this together."

"You're on your own," were Fringe's last words. She put on a big black hat that practically covered her face and slammed the door behind her.

BB and Sasha looked at each other and back at Zorro. "Now what?" asked BB. Zorro stood there stunned. "Zorro!" said BB. "What's going on?"

Sasha took over. She got down beside the shattered cabinet and starting picking up the pieces. "The first thing we do is clean up this mess. What did she mean about the owners? Doesn't the apartment belong to someone you know?"

"God, no." Zorro shook her head. "It's just an empty place. Like all of them. Somehow Master gets the keys. This time she gave the key to Fringe. But then she never showed up. I don't even know where the key is."

"Shit, Zorro," said Sasha. "Okay, I have a plan. First of all, we don't tell anyone. There's no way we can replace the cabinet. We have to make it look like a break-in. Is there a security panel or a code you used when you got here?"

"No, we let ourselves in the building using the key Fringe had. We waited until the concierge left his desk and then we came up in the freight elevator. We were wearing hoodies and turned our faces away from the security cameras."

"And there weren't any alarm systems in here?"

"No," answered Zorro.

"All right, then we clean off our fingerprints and we get out of here fast! Let the owners find this when they get home. As for us, we just pushed the buzzer code and you let us in."

"But," said BB, "Sasha and I weren't here when the damage happened. It's ridiculous that we're even doing this."

"And yet, here you are," said Zorro. She was right back into her snotty little girl act. "I like Sasha's idea. Come on, help me clean up."

After a frenzy of cleaning and bagging up the glass, the girls grabbed their purses. Zorro peeked out the door to make sure nobody was coming. As they rushed to the elevator, the doors pinged. Was the couple home so early? No, it was just a couple of teens. But the elevator and lobby were too risky. Sasha lowered her head and walked to the stairs. Zorro and BB followed. They ran down to the basement parking lot and, keeping their faces away from cameras, they headed for a nearby door.

"Slow down," said Sasha. "Nobody knows us, remember? I'll dump this plastic bag where it won't be found. We'll meet up at school tomorrow."

"Sasha," said Zorro, "thanks."

Sasha didn't look back. She let her breath out. Where did that courage come from — and the sneaky solution? She didn't want to be the leader. But if she got the CREW to trust her, it could be her way out.

✳✳✳

After a restless night, Sasha pulled herself out of bed. She wanted to meet Jake at her locker at 8:30. She really needed a friend now. BB seemed to be with her, but then again she'd spent so many years with Master . . .

When she arrived at school, there he was, standing beside her locker. His big smile made her heart beat faster. Her face smiled back without even trying. When she got there, he pecked her on the cheek.

Blushing, she said, "I've got to get my math book." She turned to her locker and worked the combination. As soon as she opened her locker, she was overwhelmed by the smell of cheap perfume. Sasha realized her whole locker had been doused with the stuff.

Everyone turned to stare as the smell wafted through the hallway. There were whispers, and someone went to notify a teacher. Soon, Frank came rushing up.

"Ms. Asinov," he said sternly. "I thought school rules were made clear to you. We have a scent-free policy here. Many students and teachers have allergies, and strong scents like this will not be tolerated."

As Sasha mumbled that she was sorry, he added, "I won't report you to the principal, because you are still new at this school. But stay here. Clear out your locker. I'll send maintenance to help you get rid of the worst of the smell."

Sasha threw the book into her locker again and slammed the door shut. "She did it," said Sasha softly. "She did it. She did it." Sasha was surprised that she felt calmer than she had all month.

"Who did it?" asked Jake.

"Nobody," she answered. "I'll take care

of this. It's just a stupid prank. Please don't mention this to anybody. Please, Jake. I don't want anyone to know about it." By now the halls were clear of students, so Sasha opened the locker again. She pulled out her books and put everything into her backpack for cleaning.

It looked like Master's jealousy was fast-tracking. Her obsession with Jake, her failing interest in the CREW, her fixation on Sasha. It was all getting worse. But if Sasha tried to expose Master now, would she just come back at her even stronger? No, Sasha had to make sure Master went down for good. And she had to do it herself.

Chapter 14

The Big Plan

"I know who did it, Jake. And I can play her game," Sasha said. "She has the power right now. But I'm going to take it from her. And when I do, she will crumble."

"You mean Martha?" said Jake. "Oh come on, she's not that powerful. I know she's got a thing for me. And I know she gets into some pretty heavy shit. But a power play like that? I don't think so. She knows she'd get into trouble."

"You don't know her. She has things on me. It's bad, Jake, really bad." Then she said, "I have to go." She left Jake standing in the middle of the stinky hall.

Her math class had already started. Master sat near the back with a smug look on her face. She caught Sasha's eye and pretended to gag. The hacking ended in a sly smile.

"Miss, I'm not feeling well, so I'm going to the nurse's office," Sasha told the teacher. The nurse wasn't in, so Sasha lay down on the cot. What she needed was time to think. But after a sleepless night, she dropped off immediately.

When Sasha finally woke up, it was after noon. She slipped out and went home. Her bed looked too good to pass up. Another nap was in order. She slept soundly until a bell in her dream kept ringing and ringing. It was the school bell and she was going to be late. She was running as fast as she could but the sun was too hot. She'd never make it in time.

Sasha woke to the late afternoon sun streaming through the window. She sat up, but the bell kept ringing. She realized it was the doorbell. Jake! She ran downstairs and threw open the door.

"Oh, thank god you are here . . ." she started. The CREW stood in the doorway.

"Thank god we're here? How nice." Master pushed past her into the living room. "Come on girls, it's time for a meeting."

Sasha ran in front of her. "You can't come in here. My mother will be home any minute." She pulled at Master's arm.

Master slapped Sasha's hand down. "Oh, I figured your mother wouldn't be home. And don't think Jake will help you. He received a text from you. It said you're not feeling well but you'd contact him when you're feeling better. Guess what? You asked him to not contact you, either."

"So you're back," Sasha said. "Where were you the other day when we needed you?"

Master shrugged. "Never mind," said Sasha. "I came up with a plan to get us out of there. Didn't I, girls?"

Zorro glared at Fringe. Fringe looked at her hands. BB moved a little closer to Sasha.

"You're not much of a 'Master' these days," Sasha continued. "Your obsession with Jake is kind of getting in the way, don't you think? Well, guess what? You can try to send me back to Russia, but my father is a very important diplomat there and will do whatever I say. And he has a lot of influence with the Canadian government. You could be in bigger trouble than me. So go ahead and try."

Master's eyebrows went up. "Aren't you cute. You think you'd make a better leader? You've been here what, two months? I have put my heart and soul into this gang, over years and years. You think you can take it away just like that? Think again. Besides, I'm not ready to give you back yet. We still have work to do. I need you, Sage. And you need me if you want to avoid a scandal. I — I mean we — can make a whole lot more money and gain more power through cybercrime than we ever could with our petty thefts and scams. We've never really been able to go there. Sage, you do that for me, and after that, we'll talk."

Master walked toward the door. "I want a BIG plan. Something that can get us a lot of money. Something to rock the world and put me on the map. I want to show the world that the CREW rules. If it works, I may let you off the hook, Sage. Free as a bird to stay or to leave us behind. But . . ." she leaned in and whispered, "there's still the Jake thing. You didn't just tell him you were sick. You 'confessed' that you staged the perfume prank so you could put more blame on me."

As soon as the girls left, Sasha called Jake. All she got was Jake's friendly voice saying, "Go with the beep." She left a hurried message.

All the drama was turning her brain to mush. She couldn't think. It would be easy to just tell Papa she wanted to come home. That she was being bullied for being Russian. She could ditch the CREW, leave Jake behind, and just go back to her life in Moscow.

But that would leave Master in charge to ruin whatever reputation Sasha had built up here. That would not please her father. Master needed to be dethroned before Sasha could live anywhere in peace. Sasha sat down and made a list of her thoughts. Slowly the fog cleared as she got everything down on paper. First of all, the Big Plan. Master wanted something big to put the CREW on the cybermap.

Second, could she trust Master to keep her promise to let her off the hook after that? Something always came up that drew Sasha in deeper. She had to figure out a way to turn the tables on Master and make it stick. Maybe the "something big" would get Sasha out of Master's grip. Maybe this was her chance turn the power around.

But it all had to be done in a way that didn't draw attention. Getting into trouble was a sure way to be sent back to Moscow.

And then there was Jake. She'd never felt this way about a guy before. She didn't want to give him up. He was mature and sensible, not like the babies she'd hung out with in Russia. But now he thought she was as unstable as Master. She couldn't drag Jake into her mess. That was a sure way to lose him.

✶✶✶

The next two weeks were exhausting for Sasha. She decided to cool it with the daily CREW demands. The excuse that she needed to concentrate on the new Big Plan got her out of meetings. And as glad as she was to see Jake at school, she understood when he didn't seem to be as glad to see her. After Master's text to him, he was probably confused about Sasha's feelings for him. Or suspected that

Sasha wasn't telling him the whole truth.

On top of all this, she had to play proper Russian diplomat daughter. She couldn't let her mother get her father more involved. But being good meant dinners out with guests and pizzas in with Mother.

Sasha needed time. Would her father help if he thought Sasha was being bullied? Bullied? How about forced into a criminal life? No, not her father. Then it came to her. She could trust Kristina, her only true friend in Moscow.

Dearest Kristina, she emailed in Russian. *I miss you so much. Friendships here are not the same as home. And now I need your help.*

Remember you said I was so strong and could handle anything in Canada? Well, there is a situation I got myself into. I am being strong but it's getting out of hand. Mother and Papa do not know this. Can we keep it to ourselves? You know how controlling they get. So here's the situation . . .

Chapter 15

First Step to Freedom

It made Sasha feel good to confess to someone she trusted. Kristina knew why Sasha had been sent away, but she'd never told anyone. Now Sasha told Kristina that her so-called friends had tricked her into something that could ruin her life. She explained about the computer help and she told her about Jake and how jealous Master was.

And now, they want to drag me into a really big scam. It will break the law in so many ways.

I don't want you to go to the police or anyone else. I just want to scare them badly. Could you send a text or two to them saying you know what they did and that you're watching them? It would probably make them give up. Can you do that?
Your best friend, Sasha

Within minutes, she received an email back.

Oh poor you, Sasha. Of course I'll do it. How's this?
"From someone you don't know and you don't want to know. We know about the computer scam and other crimes. It will cost you if you continue to pursue her. Leave Sasha alone."

Back went Sasha. *Perfect. Your English is even better than before. Here are the numbers. Let's Skype Sunday, 3 p.m. Okay?*

Yes, came the answer. *You call me.*
Sasha sent the numbers of the CREW's

secret phones. But she told Kristina to use their real names instead of their CREW identities. She figured that would scare them even more.

Satisfied that she had gained a little more time, Sasha allowed herself to come up with the Big Plan. Eating and sleeping would have to come second to that. Her mother went out most nights, so that would help. She got to work.

✱✱✱

The next night, her phone started ringing. She thought it would be Jake, so she grabbed it and answered quickly. "Hello?"

But it was just BB. "Sorry I didn't stick up for you at your house. But Master is scaring me more and more. And now I just got a text from someone who said they know everything we've done. Do you know who that is?"

Sasha responded. "Me? I don't know

anybody here except you girls. Let me look. Hey, I got one too. Did the others?"

"I don't know," said BB. "You're the first one I phoned. Wait, another text just came in. It's Zorro saying she got it. Oh shit, now Fringe.

"Wait," said BB. "Here's one from Master. She got the message too and she says this 'ups the game.' She says public CREW meetings are off for now. Here's the rest," she said, reading to Sasha. "Sage still has to give us the plan of the century. Note to Sage: In my generosity I give you two weeks more and then we'll be known around the globe. Until then, we all lie low."

As soon as she hung up, Sasha tried to reach Jake. She texted, phoned, and emailed — but nothing. It seemed her only real friend here didn't want any part of her.

Sasha wondered if she should confront Master directly about Jake. Maybe she could convince her that this rivalry was getting in the way of the Big Plan. Master was a bully, and bullies usually collapse when someone bullies back. But Sasha needed proof that Martha was behind everything if she was going to get free of the CREW. She texted Master: *This is silly. Why don't we meet alone and we can figure out how we can both get what we want. If it's Jake, let's discuss it.*

After a few minutes, Master came back with: *Well, the first sign of sanity. How about Timmy's at King and Victoria?*

Sasha responded: *I'll be there.*

Sasha set her phone to record at the subtle click of a button. She walked to the subway, thinking that if Master chose a public place to meet, maybe she was ready to really talk. If not, well, she'd at least have a recording of what went on.

At the Tim Hortons, Master was sitting at a table, waving Sasha in and smiling. *She actually can be pretty if she tries*, thought Sasha. *Why does she make herself out to be such a bitch?* But as soon as Sasha sat down, the smile vanished. Master stared at Sasha with scorn. Sasha clicked the record button on her phone in her pocket.

"So are we going to talk?" asked Sasha, trying to get Master to give up something.

Master reached in her pocket and pulled out her own phone. "This is the real reason Jake hasn't been paying much attention to you." She showed the video of Sasha morphing photos of the CREW with the guys they blackmailed. Sasha's voice was clear: "And we get them to pay — five hundred dollars a shot — to keep the pictures from their wives and bosses."

"Now, Sasha," Master said. "I can make it right. I can tell Jake that you thought it was a prank. And that you refused to take money for it. I will tell him that. After the plan is successful. Right now he thinks this is all your doing. All this is just a little incentive for you to come up with the Big Plan. And let me tell you, it better feature me front and centre."

By this time, Sasha had caught her breath. "Oh, it will," she promised. She didn't want Master to know she already had an idea in mind. First, she needed to make sure that it would work without a hitch.

"Good. For now, go home. Watch TV, do your homework, everything as usual. And, of course, create the Big Plan." Master grabbed her coffee and left.

When she got home, Sasha took a shower and had a cup of strong, sweet Russian tea. It was Mother's remedy for everything, and she needed all the help she could get. A plan had started to form in her head. Master would love it. At first.

Was she being too reckless? Her plan had three stages and it would take a lot of hard work to get it all done. Each stage was a little more risky. But if Sasha could pull it off, it would make sure everybody got something — whether they wanted it or not.

The target was Master, who loved animals.

The means, electronic — hacking into a national animal society's database. The method was a protest for animal rights. The result was money and fame for Master. And for Sasha, as it played out, the result would be revenge and freedom.

When Sasha was finally ready to present her plan, the CREW met at Master's place.

"I know Canadians love peace, children, and animals," Sasha started. "And I know that Canadians are fast to protest if one of these is in danger. Remember that scandal a week or so ago when a movie was shot in an old mine in northern Ontario?"

Sasha reminded the girls of the reports about a puppy named J.J. A secret video showed the dog being forced into water when it clearly didn't want to go. The footage went viral and animal rights had been the lead story on the news for days.

"It's time to introduce a new cyberhero to the world," said Sasha dramatically.

This is what Master was waiting for. *Cyberhero!* Sasha watched Master's face flicker through expressions as she thought about fame (wide eyes), power (straight posture), and being a cyberhero (a real smile).

Sasha went on. "This cyberhero will become known worldwide. Nothing can stop her from becoming rich and famous."

The girls all started to chatter at once. All Master could talk about was being "a new cyberhero." Her ego let her forget that Sasha was the real cyberhero. Without her, Master wouldn't go far. But Sasha was happy to wait.

Step one was in place.

Chapter 16

Fame and Fortune

Sasha created TARP — Toronto Animal Rights Protection — a fake charity. TARP's arrival on the scene would be at a protest in front of the Toronto movie studio that made the J.J. film. Sasha had hacked into the Canadian Federation of Humane Societies' database and sent invitations to thousands of animal lovers all across Canada. The media had been alerted that a nationwide animal rights protest would introduce a new cyberhero. But no details were given.

When the day arrived, Sasha moved unnoticed through the growing crowd. She took pictures of the CREW and others. Everything was on track.

By noon, five thousand people had gathered in the studio parking lot. The crowd even spilled out onto the street. When the police tried to find someone to question about a permit, there was no one who would take responsibility for organizing the event. They called the city and got confirmation that a permit for a protest for animal rights had gone out. The scribbled signature on the application looked like "T. Master." The city office did some digging and found out that the address on the form was a Tim Hortons on King Street.

Zorro, wearing a wig, sunglasses, and a big hat, stood before the crowd on a large garbage bin. She got the crowd chanting.

"Why are we here?" Zorro yelled.

"We love animals!" the crowd shouted back.

"What do we want?"

"Justice for J.J.!" As the police made their way through the crowd toward the front, Zorro jumped down from the bin and blended in with the crowd.

The crowd kept getting bigger and louder. The studio had closed for the day. But people could be seen looking through windows. A woman even came out and joined the protest. TV cameras pushed through the crowd.

At 2:00 p.m., at the peak of the protest, Zorro shouted to everyone near her to check Twitter. The first in a series of tweets, using the trending hashtag #JusticeforJJ, pleaded with the crowd to text money to TARP to help animals being used as tools for human greed. Pretty soon, everyone had seen it. The next tweet had a link to a video of animals being mistreated. It showed horses being choked to be controlled. Circus lions and tigers being whipped to perform. Dog heroes being pushed to go through wind, ice, and fire to make a good movie.

A third tweet linked an Instagram picture showing Master from the back. She wore her net body suit over a grey spandex bikini and stood with her whip ready to strike. The caption read: *The Master strikes back.*

Finally, Master appeared in a video. Her voice was disguised. But her message was clear:

"Send money to TARP now. Text the keyword 'HelpJJ' to MASTER. Your donation will help rid the world of the sick and cruel treatment of animals. More money means more help for these tortured animals. Tell your friends."

And the money poured in.

They had all agreed to meet at Master's place for debriefing that night. Munchy greeted everyone at the door with a yapping hello and a circle run. He seemed to be running off Master's energy.

Master, Zorro, and BB had watched the whole thing on the all-news station. When their retweets reached 100,000, Master applauded herself. Sasha looked on with approval. She knew every "Master" move would dig their leader in deeper.

The night called for vodka, weed, and pizza. They watched reports from on-air personalities. Their stunt was being called the most mysterious protest they'd ever covered.

"How much, Fringe?" asked Master.

"So far, forty-five thousand six hundred and fifty dollars and still coming in. Awesome! We could go to one hundred thousand."

Sasha interrupted. "I think we should close it down after a week. Between the fake permit and the media attention, somebody will track us down."

Fringe frowned. "Why close it down as long as the cash is still coming in? Shit, this could be really big."

"And it could be our lead to more than just money," added Master. "With our new 'cyberhero' leading the cause, we will become famous." The glint in Master's eye was a reminder of her real motives. "I think we'll keep this going a while. So, Sage, you just get working on the next instalment, okay?"

Sasha shook her head. "Well, it's your choice," she said. She already had the next phase well underway. "But I won't keep doing it if I think it's getting too risky. I'm the one taking the chance here. I will put the next event in place. And I'll deliver a plan for future events. When that's done, I'm done."

"Oh, look," said Fringe, ignoring Sasha. "Another thousand dollars deposited. Master, all the money has gone into the CREW's account. You decide how much we get and when."

When Master stood up, Munchy yapped in protest. Master approached Sasha, who worried for a second. But Master's words were warm. "We might not have been the best of friends until now, Sage. But this proves that you truly understand how to be CREW. I'm very proud of you."

Sasha didn't need or want Master's approval. But she had to look loyal to the

CREW, and to Master. So she smiled and hung around to celebrate with the girls.

The reports kept coming in. One reporter said, "We tried to dig up information on TARP. We found a website. But we couldn't get anything on the directors or the executive. Or, of course, the Master.

"Some people are saying this was a huge scam," the reporter went on. "But most are just happy for some good news for a change. A superhero — or, rather, a cyberhero — with good intentions. Back to you in the studio, Jackie."

✶✶✶

Jake met Sasha at their old spot at Sasha's locker the next morning.

"Was that Anzuela on that stage at the animal protest?" he asked. "Did you have something to do with that? I have to say, as soon as I saw Anzuela, I suspected the CREW. And the CREW's scams. Is it really for animal rights?"

Sasha laughed. "Oh, Jake, you have a wild imagination. I don't know anything about it. I don't think that was Anzuela. She's been busy with the CREW's normal activities."

Sasha hated lying to Jake. But she had to finish what she had started. It was the only way to make sure that Master would not bother her — or Jake — again. Still, she had to let him know that she wasn't over him.

"Look, Jake," Sasha continued. "Some things are happening in my life right now. I have to lie low. Family, school, and everything else are going to keep me out of circulation. I know Martha has told you some things about me. They're lies. You have to believe me. Anything she tells you about me is a lie. I really like you, Jake. And if you want, I'll let you know when we can start spending time together again.

"But Jake," Sasha warned. "Stay away from Martha — for your own sake."

Chapter 17

Master Woman

Soon, the attention to the animal protest story died down. It was time for stage two of Sasha's secret plan. Sasha asked to see Master alone. The next stages of her plan needed to appeal to Master's greed and vanity. And Sasha didn't want the rest of the CREW getting in the way.

The open park in the upscale area of Yorkville was Master's choice. "This place isn't my style," she told Sasha. "But I guess high-class shopping is what you're used to. I wanted you to feel comfortable."

Sasha didn't bite. "I don't really come here, either," she said. "I mostly go to the Eaton Centre for my stuff."

"It's Value Village for me." Master's smug reference to the second-hand store made Sasha feel like a snob.

Sasha laid out her latest plan. She explained that it would be more difficult to set up, but it would give Master continent-wide exposure. And it would be riskier. Sasha hoped that Master's hunger for success would lead her past the risk and into Sasha's trap.

These days Master essentially saw herself as Wonder Woman. Sasha encouraged the image of a larger-than-life character, someone whose heroic actions brought her fame and attention.

"But," Sasha told her, "to get others to see you that way, you'll have to be even bolder than you've been. Your voice has to speak directly to people who care. We need to find the people who can make a lot of noise, not just for animals, but for humans."

This time the cause was homeless girls.

A new movie was being released. It was about a teen girl who had superpowers and used them to help other young people. It was getting a lot of attention and critics loved it. It was due to open in two weeks and Sasha said she wanted to take advantage of the buzz.

The plan would bring attention to the horrors that homeless girls face. And it would strengthen Master's new role as saviour. Placing Master front and centre in a cause connected to a blockbuster movie would set Master on her way to international fame.

"But this phase is not going to bring in money," Sasha explained. This part was all about awareness. Money would come later, when they launched phase three.

"Both phases two and three are riskier," Sasha said. "They could blow up in our faces. So you'll have to trust me and follow my lead."

Master said she didn't really care about risks. Sasha knew that all Master could see was the fame, power, and love she'd always wanted when she told Sasha, "Just make it happen."

✸✸✸

It was a good thing that school work came easy for Sasha. Her schooling in Moscow gave her the discipline that got her through the next two weeks. Night and day, she put in the hours. When she felt like giving up, she thought of being free of Master. Sasha wanted to be back on a path that her father would approve of. And without Master, she would be free to be with Jake.

The movie's premiere was a huge event. In the audience were seven hundred and fifty teens, the media, and the mayor, as well as producers, directors, and actors from the movie.

Sasha had explained to Master how the plan would work. The CREW was watching Master's TV for reports. According to Sasha's plan, the movie screen would suddenly go dark. A loud voice would boom out, "We interrupt this program to alert you to a crisis. One that is going on right now!"

Thinking it was a terrorist action or a fire alarm, everyone would listen. Master would appear on the screen in her net suit and mask. In her hand would be her whip, which she would crack for attention. Sasha had written Master's message and shot the footage of her delivering it.

"Shame on all of you, sitting in your cozy seats, waiting to watch a fictional story of a superhero who saves teens.

"There's a real story about teens who need your help. When was the last time you stepped over a young girl on the street who had no place to go? Why didn't you sit down with that homeless girl? Ask about her personal story?

"These are girls on the edge. They have learning challenges. They have been abused physically, emotionally, and sexually. They have been lured to the streets by pimps. They are worse off than boys in these situations because they have been told they should give in to men.

"In this movie, someone reaches out to those in need. But real life isn't a movie. I'm here to remind you that it's up to you. You have to do it. And remember me, because I am the Master and I am calling on you to join me in this cause!"

✷✷✷

That night, the CREW met as usual. But the gathering seemed more like a funeral than a celebration. Nothing about the intervention was being reported in the news. There was no mention of the Master or a new cyberhero. Master silently paced. When Munchy came close, Master didn't stop. The brush of her foot sent Munchy crawling into a corner.

Fringe's face showed frustration. "We went too far," she said.

BB kept looking from Sasha to Master with hope. Zorro flitted around Master until

Master snapped, "The vodka's in the freezer." Glad to be doing something, Zorro ran to the kitchen and brought out supplies. She poured shots, which the CREW swallowed quickly.

Fringe headed for the door, saying she had to get home. BB quickly followed, asking Fringe for a ride. Zorro, Master's little helper, asked if it was okay to leave. Master's tight nod sent her away.

Sasha knew Master wanted to ask what went wrong. But disappointment — or maybe it was fury — held her back. So Sasha began. "Everything went as planned. I checked my files and the message was received. We all saw it on closed circuit."

"So what happened? Where's the attention? Where's the action?" Master's voice went up with each question. Then softly she said, "You failed me, Sage. Go home. We'll talk tomorrow." She picked up Munchy and went to her bedroom. The slamming of the door left Sasha alone in the worn-out room.

Chapter 18

Secret Plan

Only Sasha knew that she had not failed Master. She had turned on her. Now she had to move fast.

The next day, Sasha invited Master over to her house. She had to be very careful. Anything could go wrong. The other CREW members could get Master to see reason. Someone would check to see if the movie was really interrupted. They would question if Sasha had screwed up.

Sasha had to make sure Master listened to her and not the CREW. Besides, she wanted to protect them from the final stab. After all, they weren't all bad. They were victims of Master's ego, just like Sasha.

So Sasha would feed that ego. She would give information only Master would believe. And this time Master would be so excited about her role as an international hero, she would be willing to take chances that would expose her.

"We need to go bigger," Sasha said to Master. "You were seen by those people. I know that. They chose to ignore you. They can't do that. We've gone to too much trouble. The Master needs to be seen as a voice for special causes."

Master nodded at every point. So Sasha continued feeding Master lies that only someone obsessed would believe. "Those people in the movie saw it. But they kept it secret so they wouldn't be embarrassed by the message. These people are putting you down, Master. We can't let them get away with that."

At that, Master started pacing. She repeated under her breath, "They can't get away with it." Then she turned to Sasha. "So what do we do?"

Master was in Sasha's hands.

Sasha had made a secret plan of her own.

Step one: Take responsibility for past wrongs.

Showing a lot of shame, which she hoped Master would believe, Sasha said, "I was wrong before, I admit it. We need to stick to those who believe in our causes. That's what worked at the protest. We need to get your fans back to you. My fault."

Master was nodding.

Step two: Offer hope.

"So this time," Sasha said, "we start at

home. We build a base of those who will follow you anywhere. Using animal rights and homeless girls as our causes, we put you in front of an audience who cares."

Sasha went on, "The Master needs to become a big-name cyberhero. Someone speaking out for the little guy. You've started that. Next, you add your fans' strength to yours. That will convince the people who make the rules to change the rules. By then, the Master will be so powerful, they won't be able to ignore you anymore."

Master was almost hooked. She leaned close to Sasha to hear every word.

Step three: Solve the problem.

"Now, here's what we do," Sasha said. She explained that an important part of the plan was to cut off the rest of the CREW, just for a while. "They can't do anything, anyway. I'm afraid they'll just get in the way. Together, you and I can show the world the real Master."

By now, Master was all in. The making of *the Master* was the priority. "The CREW will understand," she said.

"Everything is in place for two days from now. Be ready."

The event was Superior Girls day. It was a global event that showed off the strengths of teen girls and the projects they'd made happen. A rock concert was scheduled for the biggest outdoor venue in the city. Twenty-five thousand tickets had been sold and the concert would be streamed to ten countries worldwide. A screening was set up in their school gym. All the schools in the area had been invited, and their school would showcase local talent too.

At 7:00 p.m. Toronto time, the concert started on the big stage with a mini fireworks display. There were explosions, laser lights, and a lot of noise. Famous girl performers lined the stage. Their appearance prompted screams from audiences around the globe. The buzz in the school gym matched those at the concert.

At exactly 7:12 p.m., the Master walked onto the school stage. Her image was complete with her net suit and whip. Everyone in the audience fell silent. They looked at one another. Staff and organizers checked their programs and schedules. They found nothing to explain the interruption. The tech person paused the playing of the screening.

On stage, in person, Master looked small. There was nothing heroic about her. She looked like a cartoon character, not someone who was about to rule the world.

Security hurried to the stage to pull off the intruder. They were met by loud opposition from the crowd.

"No, that's the Master," someone called out. "Let's hear how she is going to save the world."

"I saw her on YouTube. She's wild," another shouted.

"What is it thou wants, oh Master?" A boy fell to his knees and pretended to grovel.

The mockery was not lost on Master. But she went with the script anyway. "I want to save the world from cruelty, homelessness, abuse, and neglect," she said. But the power of the previous video was missing. And she forgot that her low, distinctive voice could be recognized. A couple of girls whispered and pointed.

Someone in the crowd jumped on the stage and grabbed a mic. "Ladies and gentlemen, I present the Master. She was just telling everyone that she is going to save the world. Check it out. It's on a video of her that is being replayed on the all-news station."

When they looked at the posted video on their phones, the crowd saw the clip Sasha had shot of Master. But there was nothing about homeless teen girls. All it showed was Master cracking her whip and crowing, "I am the Master. Watch for more!"

On the stage, Master held her arms in the air and swung her whip.

The crowd went wild. But instead of cheering, they were laughing and booing.

"The saviour — like Jesus Christ or Buddha?"

"Master? More like disaster!"

"Love your outfit. Didn't I see you at Milly's strip club?"

"No!" shouted Master. Her voice was getting more unsure by the minute. "I can lead you to do more. Follow me and we'll help those whom the world rejects."

"Hey, wait," shouted one girl. "She sounds like Martha. Martha, what *are* you doing up there?"

Master could see that she was being ridiculed, not adored. She tried to get the crowd back, but the fury was gone. All that was left was defeat.

Finally, security guards made their way through the mayhem and grabbed her. She collapsed in their hold and was dragged off the stage.

The crowd kept booing and laughing. But soon they remembered what they were there for and started calling for the real show. After a few minutes, BB walked slowly onto the stage. She just stood there until the audience went silent.

"You're here to see a show — a great show," she started.

There was cheering and calls for "let's do it!"

"And you will see a great show," BB went on. "But I'd like to take a moment to ask you not to mock Martha. We've all known her for a long time — some of us since grade seven. To us, the CREW, she is Master. Over the years, she has watched over strays like us, even though her own life has been completely unstable and wretched."

BB's voice rose. "She's been under a lot of stress lately. So her methods are maybe a little off the wall. But the message is real. Superior girls can save the world," she shouted.

Sasha held her breath. She listened to the silence that stretched to the back of the gym. *Come on. Come on!* she thought.

Suddenly, the place erupted with cheers and applause. Programs were thrown in the air and the stomping began again. There were no boos, no laughing this time.

Sasha let out her breath and cheered with the others. BB left the stage and the screen flipped back to the concert.

Chapter 19

Family First

Master was arrested for disturbing the peace. While she was waiting to get out on bail, the CREW met one more time — this time in Sasha's home. The gang's loyalty to Master was quickly forgotten. They turned to Sasha as their leader. Fringe and Zorro started to present ideas to her for more scams and more crimes.

But Sasha didn't want it. She wanted to get out. She not only needed to stop herself from committing more crimes, but also to rid herself of the temptation. She'd always protested against doing the things Martha demanded. But she knew she was open to creative chances to use her computer skills. She knew sticking with the CREW would pull her in again.

Fringe gave a report on their secret account. "We have more than fifty thousand dollars in our account. Should we split it?" she asked hopefully.

Sasha watched the reactions. Zorro raised her eyebrows in interest. BB looked at Sasha for guidance. "What about you, Sage?" BB asked.

"I don't want any part of that money," said Sasha. "And my name is Sasha, not Sage. If we're smart, we'll all go back to our real names. We need to get back to reality."

"About the money, though," Sasha went on. "My portion goes to the Canadian Federation of Humane Societies."

"But . . ." Frances whined. Sasha cut her off with a shrug.

"I suggest letting it all go and giving it to our causes — the Humane Societies and groups that provide support to homeless girls. Then we can all start fresh with no suspicious money tied to us. And no ties to Master — or Fringe, or Zorro, or BB. Or Sage. I can make sure any connections to the frauds disappear."

Anzuela smirked. "Do we give the pervs back their money?"

"No!" shouted Frances. "Not that. They deserved that. Give their portion to the dogs."

Everyone laughed.

***

Two weeks after the last CREW meeting, Jake and Sasha ran into each other outside of school. They had cooled it for so long they found it hard to know what to say. After the outing of Master on the school stage, Sasha felt she owed Jake an explanation. She knew it might turn him off forever. But she had to tell the truth. Sasha confessed to the cybercrimes. She also admitted that she was the one who took down the CREW.

Standing on the street corner, Jake said, "That sounds good for you, Sasha. I'm happy for you. But I have to tell you, I need some time to sort out my feelings for you. And to figure out what I think about your extracurricular skills and the trouble they could get you into."

Attracted as Sasha still was to Jake, she understood. She told him she would give him whatever space he needed. "You know where to reach me," she said.

And her world slowly went back to normal.

After a week Jake texted: *Can we meet? Camp Café at 4 p.m.?*

Sasha immediately sent back: *Yes!*

After an awkward greeting, Sasha asked Jake how he'd been doing. She knew the school had just won a citywide basketball tournament, and she was excited to focus on him, on ordinary life.

But when she tried to talk about it, Jake interrupted. "Well, mostly I've been thinking about you."

Sasha's voice caught in her throat. "Me?" she croaked.

"Yeah," he said, "maybe we could start fresh. I mean — not forgetting everything that has happened. But getting past it. What do you think?"

Sasha took his hand and smiled. "Yes." Maybe Jake could go back to seeing Sasha the way he first saw her — as a smart, beautiful girl who was looking for friends in a new country.

But Sasha kept thinking about Master — or Martha. She wondered if she was okay. Master might have been bad, or even evil. But Martha had been a huge influence in Sasha's first months in Canada. Sasha talked herself into the idea that seeing Martha would bring closure for her. She had to see her former adversary face-to-face one more time.

Martha was living in a halfway house for people who had broken the law. As the cab brought Sasha to the front doors, she couldn't help but compare the place to the seniors' residence. Inside there was a hint of lemon, but no pee and vegetables. Sasha was grateful that Martha was somewhere like this. It was likely nicer than anywhere Martha had ever lived.

To Sasha's surprise, Martha greeted her with a hug. But she pulled back quickly. "Hey," Martha said. "Come on, we can talk outside."

As always, Martha took the lead. Sasha followed her to a garden where people were strolling and sitting on benches. It was like a public park. Martha walked over to a bench out of the sun and sat down. She was wearing a thin grey hoodie and faded jeans. Gone were the uniform and the Master costume.

Sasha wondered how to start. What should she say? "Master . . ." Sasha began.

"Oh, please." Master waved her hand. "It's Martha. That Master stuff is over."

"Okay, Martha. I didn't know whether to come or not. I didn't know if you'd want to see me after all we've been through. Like . . . I mean, I don't even know what to say to you now that we're here."

Martha just sat there looking at the trees and plants. Finally she said in her smoky voice, "You know, Sage, you and I aren't so different. I know you felt the high as much as I did. Even though you always said you did it to get out of a tight spot."

Sasha reminded herself: *Manipulation. Watch out.* She would not be sucked in again.

"I'm glad you're out of that life," said Sasha. "I am too. But I think we're very different. We don't have the same need for the thrill. I'm making new friends — real friends who see me for myself. I'm going to a new school in the fall too." She stood up. "And I'm sorry, but I won't be back."

Martha's pretty face dropped. Then she stood up too. "Well, my probation says I can't spend time with any members of the CREW, so I took a chance here. I appreciate your coming, though."

She gave a little finger wave and left the garden.

On the way home Sasha thought about the visit. Was Martha right? Would Sasha's need to push the limits allow her to straighten up? Her crimes did escalate once she got to Canada. Was her connection to the CREW important to her because she needed new friends? Or because as a gang they lived on the edge?

Well, Sasha thought, *a new year, a new school and new friends will bring what it will bring*. In the end she decided she was ready for a change.

Sasha's dad was arriving that weekend. And he had a new position that would keep him in Canada. Sasha's mother had announced proudly:

"I will be the wife of the next Russian consul in Toronto." As usual, it was all about her.

Sasha realized she really wanted to see her father. When Sasha Skyped with him, he said, "You've done well, *kotyonok moya*. And for that I will give you a nice little city car to get back and forth from your new school."

Sasha felt a bit guilty about her year of crime. She protested, "But Papa, I don't need that. I always take the bus. Besides, I haven't done that well."

"Alexandra Asinov," he said. When he used her full name, it was serious. "I know you are not an angel. Neither am I. But I'm coming to Canada to be different. Maybe all of us can start fresh together. It was a mistake to separate the family. We need each other for support. So it's to make sure you can get home every day. And to let you go and come freely with my confidence that you will do the right thing. I want you to have the car."

Sasha could feel the tears starting to bubble in her eyes. "I love you, Papa. And I'll make you proud."

Sasha and her mother visited Sasha's new private girls' school on Mount Pleasant Road. Sasha thought it was okay. The uniforms and rules were a little stiff. But the admissions staff had heard about her computer skills and offered her a job setting up a computer course for the senior girls. It was a little scary. Was Sasha the best person to be in charge of computers and other girls?

On the other hand, she thought it might be what she needed. This could help her to completely rid herself of the CREW. If ordinary friends needed ordinary computer help, she could give it. And who said a gang had to be involved in crime?

11/18

Acknowledgements

First and foremost, I acknowledge the support of my husband, Bob, who is always there for me. I also thank Ontario Arts Council who provided the means for me to get my first traditionally published book out there.

I also want to thank my editor, Kat Mototsune, for her guidance and assistance. She was always patient with me and I do appreciate it.